## "My name is Cesar DeSanquez."

DeSanquez, DeSanquez... Annie was thinking frowningly. And then it hit—with a sickening sense of understanding that made her sway where she stood.

"Ah," he murmured. "I see you are beginning to catch on. You made the quick connection, I must assume, because your...affair with my brother-in-law took place in the DeSanquez apartment. The media made quite a meal out of these juicy facts, did they not? They told of Annie Lacey lying with her lover in one bed, while her lover's wife lay asleep in another bedroom in the same apartment. My apartment, Miss Lacey," he enunciated thinly. "My bed!"

Dear Reader,

Welcome to a new year, and a compulsive and exciting new series in Presents: FORBIDDEN! These are stories in which romance shouldn't happen—but, luckily for us, it does!

This month, top Presents author Michelle Reid takes you to the edge with *The Morning After*, a tale of passion and revenge, and then delights you with the happiest of endings. Michelle is British, living in Manchester, England, and says that she often writes at her best during the early hours of the morning, when everyone else is asleep!

Enjoy our little taste of FORBIDDEN! and look out for another great title in this series next month.

Sincerely,

The Editor

# MICHELLE REID

## The Morning After

**Harlequin Books**

TORONTO • NEW YORK • LONDON
AMSTERDAM • PARIS • SYDNEY • HAMBURG
STOCKHOLM • ATHENS • TOKYO • MILAN
MADRID • WARSAW • BUDAPEST • AUCKLAND

ISBN 0-373-11859-7

THE MORNING AFTER

First North American Publication 1997.

Copyright © 1996 by Michelle Reid.

# CHAPTER ONE

ANNIE wanted to scream. She *tried* to scream! But every time she opened her mouth he covered it with his own.

It was horrible. A violation. She felt sick.

And it was dark in the room—very dark. The air hot and stifling, filled with the laboured breathing of their uneven struggle. Hands grappling against intrusive hands—her strangled sobs mingling with his thick, excited groans. Alien sounds, smells and textures swamping her senses to hold her trapped in a terrifyingly black void of wretched helplessness.

Suffocating—she felt as if she was suffocating. She couldn't breathe. She couldn't think beyond that vile, thrusting tongue. She could feel her heart pounding in wild fear. It throbbed in her chest, her head—thundered in her ears.

Her clothes had gone. She didn't know where or even how they had gone—but they were no longer covering her body.

Louis Alvarez was. Big, strong and repulsively naked. His greedy hands touching everywhere—*everywhere*.

It didn't help that she was slightly drunk from the amount of champagne that she had swallowed. She felt weak and dizzy, her head swimming as she tossed it from side to side in an effort to evade his awful mouth.

He dealt with this by reaching out to grasp a fistful of her silken gold hair, using it to clamp her twisting head to the bed. Her whimper of pain brought his smothering mouth back onto hers.

And then the real nightmare began.

His free hand, shifting to cover one madly palpitating breast, moulding, squeezing before moving on, palm sliding over quivering flesh, eager, hungry. Fingers searching, probing, hurting until, on a sudden surge of sexual urgency, he thrust a knee between her thighs and wedged them wide apart.

Then he was there, heavy on her, his mouth dragging sideways away from hers on a rasping sigh of pleasure as his swollen manhood made contact with her warm flesh.

And at last from somewhere—from nowhere—she didn't know where—she found the ability to scream. Her body arching away from the invading thrust of his body, her slender neck arching away from the sickening threat of his thrusting tongue—

Then a door was opening, a burst of light flooding like acid through her tortured mind. And the scream came, thick and wretched—a cry from hell, filling the air around her...

The flash bulbs began popping even before the limousine drew to a halt outside the hotel. Annie Lacey and Todd Hanson were big news at the moment. And the paparazzi were out in force.

The car stopped, a uniformed attendant stepped forward to open a door and the flash bulbs went wild, catching frame by frame the appearance of a strappy gold shoe and one long, long silk-clad female leg. Then a head appeared, breast-length, die-straight wheat-blonde hair floating around a physically perfect female face, followed by the rest of the exquisite creature, wearing nothing more than a shimmering short scrap of pure white silk that seemed held to her body only by the thin gold belt she had cinched into her narrow waist.

Annie Lacey. Tall, blonde and leggy. A lethal combination. Beautiful, with a pair of cool, cool pure blue eyes which were so disconcertingly at odds with her shockingly sensual siren's mouth. She was the present-day super-sought-after supermodel. And super-tramp to those who believed slavishly every word printed by the tabloid Press.

They envied her, though. Love or despise her for her morals, they envied her how she looked and what those looks had brought her.

Fame. Fortune.

Gods, to a lot of people. Unreachable dreams to most. To Annie herself?

Well, she used that gorgeous mouth to smile for the cameras while those blue eyes gave nothing away of what was going on behind them. What Annie thought or felt about most things was kept a close secret—which was why the Press had such a field-day where she was concerned. They could say and print what they liked about her, safe in the knowledge that she wouldn't retaliate.

Smile and say nothing, was her motto. Because whatever you did say would be taken down and twisted into something completely different—mainly something more likely to sell papers. And that meant lies, sex and the inevitable scandal—a lesson she had once learned the hard way.

A man—a big, blond-haired, blue-eyed man who was as handsome as she was beautiful—rounded the car to arrive at her side, and instantly the media interest intensified.

'Mr Hanson—Mr Hanson! It is true that Annie got the *Cliché* contract as a direct result of her relationship with you?'

Todd's hand settled about Annie's waist, drawing her close as the next question hit.

'Are you lovers, Mr Hanson?'

'Will Susie Frazer return to the States now she's lost both you and the *Cliché* contract, Mr Hanson?'

'Is there any truth in the rumour that Miss Frazer dumped you because you refused to dump Miss Lacey?'

'I hate you for setting us both up for this,' Annie threw at Todd through gritted teeth.

'Just keep smiling and ignore them,' was all he replied, pressing her into motion towards the hotel. 'They're just fishing. They don't really know anything.'

'What, with Susie feeding them their lines?' she drawled.

'She's a bitch,' he allowed, 'but not that big a bitch.'

'Was that a joke?' Annie mocked him. 'She's out for blood. My blood preferably.'

'I wish you two could have become friends,' he sighed as they stepped through the hotel doors.

'And pigs might fly,' was her only reply to that.

There never had been any love-loss in evidence between the two top models from the moment they'd first met. That had been just over six months ago, when Susie Frazer had come to London from her native Los Angeles to attend the British Advertising Awards.

Annie had been there with Todd that time too, he in his role as head of Hanson Publications and more specifically as representative of *Cliché* magazine—one of the top British monthly glossies on the present-day market—and Annie because she was featured in that month's issue of *Cliché* wearing that season's latest from the Paris shows.

Susie had taken one look at the dynamically handsome Todd Hanson and fallen like a ton of bricks—had seen that he had none other than the notorious Annie Lacey hanging on his arm and declared outright war on the spot.

'Who does she think she is, looking at you as if you're dirt?' Todd had demanded furiously.

'My reputation goes before me, darling,' she'd drawled mockingly in reply. 'But, you have to admit, she does look rather spectacular glaring at me like that.'

Tall and reed-thin, the brilliant flame of her gorgeous red hair forming the most wonderful halo of fire around her exquisite face, spectacular Susie certainly had looked. And despite his anger Annie had been able to tell by the sudden gleam in his eye that Todd had thought so too. So she hadn't been that surprised to discover a few weeks later that Susie had moved into Todd's apartment with him.

LUCKY DEVIL HANSON HAS THE PICK OF THE CROP! the tabloids had read that week, featuring accompanying photos of Todd with Annie and Todd with Susie, both women gazing adoringly into his handsome face. Annie had thought it rather amusing, but Susie hadn't. She was spoiled, vain, jealous and possessive. And she wanted Annie cut right out of Todd's life. The fact that she had never managed to achieve this aim made her animosity towards Annie almost palpable. So when Annie had been chosen over Susie to promote *Cliché's* launch into Europe earlier this week Susie had retaliated by walking out on Todd.

Which was why Annie was here tonight with Todd, instead of Susie. He was still stinging from the way that Susie had walked out on him, and his self-esteem had hit rock-bottom. He needed a beautiful woman hanging on his arm to bolster his ego and—no vanity intended— Annie was undoubtedly it!

'Susie will be there,' he'd said, explaining his reason for wanting her here with him tonight. 'She's accused me often enough of having something going with you. So let her think she was right! It will certainly hit her where it will hurt her the most—in her over-suspicious little mind!'

It hadn't been the best incentive that Annie had ever been offered to attend something she did not want to go to. But what the heck? she'd decided ruefully; her own reputation had been shot to death years ago when she'd been named as the other woman in the much publicised Alvarez divorce. And Annie owed Todd—owed him a lot for bringing her through that wretched ordeal a reasonably sane woman.

Like the rock she had always likened him to. Todd had stood by her right through it all, not caring if some of her dirt rubbed off on him. But, most precious of all, he'd believed her—believed her in the sight of so much damning evidence against her, and for that she would always be grateful. Grateful enough to do anything for him—even play the outright vamp if he asked it of her.

Which was exactly what she was here to do. But...

'Just remember I'm here only as a big favour to you,' she reminded him as they paused in the open doorway to the huge reception room to take in the glittering array of those already gathered there, who were considered best and most powerful in the advertising fraternity. 'Once I'm sure Susie has taken note that we are a pair I'm off home. I hate these kinds of do's.'

But, champagne glass in hand, she moved with Todd from group to group, smiling, chatting, smoothly fielding the light and sometimes not so light banter came their way, and generally giving the impression that she was thoroughly enjoying herself, while her eyes kept a sharp look-out for Susie.

It was then that she felt it—a sharp, tingling sensation in her spine that caught at her breath and made her spin quickly to search out the originator of the red-hot needles at present impaling themselves in her back.

She expected to see Susie. In fact, she had been so sure it would be Susie that it rather disconcerted her to find herself staring across the crowded room at not a red-haired witch with murderous green eyes but a man. A strange man. The most darkly attractive man she had ever encountered in her life before.

Dressed in a conventional black bow-tie and dinner suit, he stood a good head and shoulders taller than anyone else. His hair was black—an uncompromising raven-black, dead straight and shiny, scraped severely back from a lean, darkly tanned face. A riveting face. A face with eyes that seemed to be piercing right into her from beneath the smooth black brows he had lowered over them. Thin nose, straight, chiseled mouth and chin—he had the haughty look of a Spanish conquistador about him. And he possessed the neat, tight body of a dancer, slim but muscled, lithe like a dancer—a Spanish dancer, she found herself extending hectically.

Something like a small explosion of feeling took place deep inside her stomach, and hurriedly she looked away, going to wind herself closer to Todd, as though his reassuring bulk could soothe the disturbing sensation away.

'What's the matter with you?' Todd murmured, turning from the conversation he was having with a couple of business cronies to frown at the way she was suddenly clinging to his arm.

'Nothing,' she denied, feeling decidedly agitated. 'Where's Susie?' she snapped with a sudden impatience. 'I would have thought she'd have shown her face by now.'

Todd smiled—a thin, hard parody of a smile. 'She's over there,' he said, nodding his head in the direction in which Annie had just seen the stranger. 'Playing vamp to that guy from the Rouez Sands Group.'

'Who—Josh Tulley?'

'Mmm,' he confirmed, hiding his jealousy behind that casual reply.

But Annie wasn't fooled. She knew how crazy Todd was about Susie. She knew how much this was hurting him, and her eyes clouded in gentle sympathy. 'You have been living like man and wife for the last six months, darling,' she reminded softly. 'Maybe she has a right to feel rejected by you over this *Cliché* thing.'

If Annie had been hoping that her defence of Susie would help soften his heart towards the woman he loved, it didn't. If anything it only helped to annoy him. 'I'm a businessman, not a pimp,' he clipped. 'My boardroom is not in my bedroom. She knew that before she decided to try her luck in either.'

But that is not what the papers are saying, is it? Annie contemplated heavily. And once again it would be Annie Lacey who was going to carry the mucky can. Then she was instantly disgusted with herself for worrying about her own bad press when Todd had not worried about the mud thrown at him during her fall from grace four years ago!

'Love you,' she murmured softly, and reached up to press a tender kiss to his cheek.

Then she almost fell over when those red-hot needles returned with a vengeance. They prickled her spine, raising the fine, silken hairs on the back of her neck, drying her mouth, tightening tiny muscles around her lungs so that she found breathing at all an effort.

She must have actually stumbled because suddenly Todd exclaimed, 'What the hell—?' He made a grab to steady her, his blue eyes narrowing into a puzzled frown as he peered down into her unusually flushed face. 'Are you tipsy?' he demanded, sounding almost shocked.

It was a shock she well understood. Todd knew as well as Annie did that she had not consumed more than half a glass of anything alcoholic in any one evening in over four years.

Not since the Alvarez affair, in fact.

She shuddered on the name. 'No. I just feel a bit flushed, that's all.' Hamming it up, she began fanning herself with a hand. 'It's so damned hot in here. Oh, look! There's Lissa!' she cried, wanting to divert him. Why, she wasn't sure. 'I'll leave you to your boring businessmen and go and have a chat. Is Susie still in evidence?'

Todd glanced over Annie's shoulder then away again swiftly. 'Yes,' he said, and she could tell by the sudden tensing of his jaw that he hadn't liked what he'd seen.

'Then I want a kiss,' Annie commanded, reaching up to wind her arms around his neck.

He grinned, relaxing again, and gave it.

'Take that, you bitch,' she murmured to the unseen Susie as they drew apart.

Todd shook his head with a wry smile of appreciation for the act that she was putting on for him. 'You,' he murmured, 'are a dangerous little witch, Annie Lacey.'

'Because I love you and don't mind showing it?' she questioned innocently.

'No,' he chuckled. 'Because you love me one way but enjoy presenting it in another. Now, stop laying it on with a trowel and go and talk to Lissa.'

He gave her a light tap on her rear to send her on her way and she fluttered her lashes at him as she went, his laughter following behind her.

The sound was like manna from heaven to Annie, who hadn't heard him laugh like that in days. And she decided it was worth all the speculative looks that she was now receiving from those around them who had witnessed their little staged scene just to know that he had got his sense of humour back.

And that included the dark, brooding look that she was receiving from one man in particular, she noted on a sudden return of that hot breathlessness.

He was now standing on the other side of the room—though how he'd got there that quickly through this crush Annie didn't know.

Her heart skipped a beat.

That look was very proprietorial.

Who did he think he was, looking at her like that?

Her chin came up, her famous, cool blue eyes challenging him outright.

He smiled, his chiselled mouth twisting wryly, and he gave a small shrug of one broad shoulder as if to say, I have no right but—what the hell?

Arrogant devil! With a toss of her beautiful hair she spun away and went to join her agent. But right through the next half-hour she was acutely aware of him, what he was doing and who he was talking to.

And even more acutely aware of every time his glance came her way.

It was weird, oddly threatening yet disturbingly intimate.

Todd joined her, and after a short while they moved off through the crush, eyes with varying expressions following their slow progress as they paused several times to speak to people they knew. Some envied Todd Hanson the delicious woman curved to his side, and some envied her the attractive man she was with. But few could deny that they complemented each other perfectly—she with her long, softly rounded, very feminine body, he with his tightly packed, muscled frame, both with their fair-skinned, blond-haired, aggravatingly spectacular looks.

They ended up in another room where a buffet had been laid out. It was the usual kind of spread expected at these functions—finger food, high on calories and low on appetite satisfaction. Todd loaded up a plate with Annie's help, then they found a spot against a wall to share their spread, the plate full of food balanced between them on the flat of Todd's palm.

It all looked very cosy, very intimate, with Todd feeding Annie her favourite devilled prawns while she held a chicken drumstick up for him to bite into. But the conversation between them was far from cosy.

'Well, did you get to speak to her?' Annie asked him bluntly.

'She collared me.' Todd shrugged offhandedly. 'It wasn't the other way around.'

'After waiting until I was safely out of the way, of course. Bite—you've missed a tasty bit there...' He bit, sharp white teeth slicing easily into succulent chicken. 'So, what did she have to say?'

Another shrug. 'Nothing worth repeating,' he dismissed.

Which meant, Annie surmised, that Susie had spent the time she'd had alone with him slaying Annie's character. He fed her a mushroom-filled canapé and she chewed on it thoughtfully for a while, then said firmly, 'All right, tell me what you said to her, then.'

For a moment his eyes twinkled, wry amusement putting life into the pure blue irises. 'Just like that,' he murmured ruefully. 'She could just have been enquiring about your health, you know.'

'And we both know she was not,' Annie drawled.

He huffed out a short laugh. 'Do you have any false illusions about yourself at all, Annie?' he asked curiously.

'None that I know of.' She pouted, then, like him, shrugged a slender shoulder. 'They wouldn't be much use to me if I did have them, would they?' She was referring to the fact that people believed what they were conditioned to believe, and the Alvarez affair had done the conditioning on her character four years ago.

His blue eyes clouded at her candid honesty about herself, a grim kind of sympathy replacing the moment's amusement. 'I wish...' he began, but she stopped him by placing sticky fingers over his lips.

'No,' she said, her eyes suddenly dark and sombre. 'No wishes. No heart-searching or self-recriminations. They serve no useful purpose. And we know what we are to each other, no matter what everyone else wants to believe.'

'I love you,' he murmured, and kissed the tips of her fingers where they lay lightly against his mouth.

'Now that,' she decided, 'has just earned you the right to use me whenever you want to. Business or pleasure, my love. I am at your service!'

A sudden movement on the very periphery of her vision had her head twisting in that direction just in time to catch sight of her stranger turning away from them, and that odd feeling went chasing down her spine again.

'Have you any idea who that man is?' she asked Todd.

'Which one?' he prompted, glancing in the direction that she was looking, but already the stranger had disappeared through the door which led into the main function room.

'It doesn't matter.' She turned back to face Todd. 'He's gone.' And she made a play of cleaning her sticky fingers on the damp towels provided, aware that Todd was frowning at her, wondering why she'd felt driven to remark on the person at all. He knew that it wasn't like her; she usually showed a distinct lack of interest in the male sex in general. So her sudden interest in one man in particular intrigued him. But just when he was going to quiz her further a colleague of his joined them, and the moment was lost.

A fact for which Annie was thankful, because she didn't think that she could give Todd a reason why the stranger was bothering her as much as he was. He was impertinent, certainly. The way he had been watching her all evening made him that. And arrogant too, because he didn't even bother to look away when she caught him doing it!

But...

She had no answer to her 'but'. And on a sudden burst of restlessness she excused herself from Todd and his companion with the excuse that she was going to the bathroom.

She began threading her way through the crowd towards the main foyer, a tall, graceful mover with the kind of figure that was now back in fashion—slender but curvy, with high, firm breasts, a narrow waist and sensually rounded hips.

Being so blonde meant that the white and gold combination of her outfit suited her, the silk clinging sensually as she walked, advertising the distinct lack of underwear beneath it. But although she was well aware of the admiring glances that she was receiving she acknowledged few of them, smiling only at people she knew but giving them no chance to waylay her.

The foyer was almost as busy as the function rooms, with people milling about or just standing in small groups chatting, and Annie paused by the doorway, her blue gaze searching for the direction of the ladies' room. She spied it way across on the other side of the thickly carpeted foyer, but had barely taken a small step in that direction when she caught a flashing glimpse of flamered hair and sighed when she realised that Susie was going in the same direction.

In no mood for a cat-fight in the Ladies, she watched Susie disappear from view, then turned, feeling a bit at a loss as to what to do next and wondering if she dared just walk out of here without telling Todd.

She'd had enough now and wanted to go home. The tall dark stranger had unsettled her. And the fact that Todd had already had his confrontation with Susie, and that Susie was completely aware of whom Todd was here with, made her reasons for being here at all redundant.

And, to be honest, her bed beckoned. In her line of business early nights were a fact of life, and her body clock was telling her that she was usually tucked up and fast asleep by now.

Quite how it happened she didn't know, but all of a sudden a noisy group came bursting out of the room she'd just left, forcing her to take a quick step back out of their way—which brought her hard up against the person standing behind her.

She turned quickly to apologise—only to stiffen on a fiercely indrawn breath as something icy cold and very wet landed against her chest...!

# CHAPTER TWO

'OH . . .!' she gasped out shrilly.

'Damn,' a deep voice muttered. 'My apologies.'

But Annie was too busy trying to catch her breath to listen to any apology as she watched what looked like the full contents of a tall, fluted glass of champagne drip down the honeyed slopes of her breasts. Ice-cold bubbles were fizzing against her heated skin, the chilled liquid soaking into the thin white silk of her bodice.

The fabric darkened, then turned transparent before her very eyes, plastering itself so tightly to her breasts that anyone within a vicinity of ten feet would now know that she was definitely not wearing a bra! And to top that humiliating exposure her nipples, always so annoyingly sensitive to quick changes in temperature, burst into tight, prominent buds, pushing against the wet fabric in sheer, affronted surprise!

'Hell,' the culprit muttered, making her wretchedly aware that he was seeing exactly what she was seeing— and from a better vantage point than anyone else, including herself. In a delayed act of modesty she snapped her arms across her breasts at the same time as her head came up to receive the second stunning shock in as many seconds.

It was the man who had been watching her all evening—the same man who had filled her with such strange, unsettling feelings—and she just stared at him blankly, her lovely mouth parted while her body quivered badly enough for anyone to see that she was suffering from a severe state of shock.

Then flash bulbs began to pop, and the next thing she knew a male chest of a rock-like substance was blocking her off from view as a strong arm whipped around her waist to pull her hard up against his muscle-packed frame.

'Pretend you know me!' he muttered urgently. And before she could begin to think what he meant his mouth took fierce possession of her own.

Annie froze, this shock invasion, coming on top of all the other shocks she had just received, holding her so stiff and still that she simply let him get away with it!

But the shock did not stop her from being intensely aware of the way his mouth seemed to burn against her own, or the way he was holding her so tightly that her wet breasts were being crushed against the silky fabric of his dinner jacket. And she could feel his breath warm against her cheek, smell the slightly spicy scent of him that teased her stammering senses.

She was panting for breath by the time he drew away, giving only enough space between their lips so he could speak to her softly and swiftly. 'At the moment only you and I know about the champagne.' His voice held the finest hint of an accent—American tinged with something else . . . 'Keep up the pretence of knowing me and those greedy cameras will merely believe that Annie Lacey has just been greeted by one of her many lovers. You understand?'

Many lovers? She blinked, still too shocked, too bewildered by a mad set of events to begin to think clearly.

Then more flash bulbs popped, and she closed her eyes as tomorrow's headlines played their acid taunt across the inside of her lids: ANNIE LACEY BARES ALL IN CHAMPAGNE CLASH!

'Oh, God,' she whispered shakily.

He shifted slightly, accepting her response as acknowledgement of his advice, a large hand splaying across the base of her spine to ease her more closely to him. 'Smile,' he instructed brusquely.

Obediently she fixed a tight, bright smile to her throbbing lips.

'Now reach up and kiss me in return.'

Her eyes widened, then darkened in dumb refusal. He read it, and his own eyes flashed a warning. Green, she realised quite out of context. His eyes were green.

'Do it!' he commanded harshly. 'Do it, you fool, if you want this to look natural!'

More flash bulbs popped, congealing the horror in her shock-paralysed throat when she realised that her choices were few. She either complied with this frightening man's instructions or she faced the humiliation that she would receive at the hands of the gutter Press.

It was no contest really, she decided bleakly. The Press would be cruel—too cruel. This man—this frightening stranger—could never hurt her as deeply as a ruthless Press could do.

So with a dizzy sense of unreality washing numbly through her, her eyes clinging like confused prisoners to the glinting urgency in his, her tense fingers began sliding up his chest and over his broad shoulders, and her slender body stretched up along the ungiving length of his as she went slowly up on tiptoe to bring her reluctant mouth into contact with his.

Only, her mouth never made it as she received yet another shock—a shock which made her wet breasts heave against his hard chest in surprise, and sent her blue eyes wider, her quivering mouth too—when her fingers made accidental contact with something at his nape.

His hair was so long that he had it tied back with a thin velvet ribbon!

He gave a soft laugh deep in his throat, white teeth flashing between beautifully moulded lips, sardonically smiling in amusement at her shock.

Then he wasn't smiling, his green eyes darkening into something that stung her with a hot, dark sense of her own femininity and had her body stiffening in rejection even as he arched her up against him and closed the gap between their mouths.

She stopped breathing. Her fingers coiled tensely around that long, sleek tail of dark, silken hair as fine, pulsing jets of stinging, hot awareness sprayed heat across her trembling flesh.

For all her carefully nurtured reputation, for all the juicy rumours about her personal life, Annie rarely allowed herself to be properly kissed, rarely let any man close enough to try—though those who wished to would rather have died than admit such a thing to anyone, which was why her image as a man-killer stayed so perfectly intact.

So to have this man kiss her—not superficially but with enough sensual drive to have her own lips part to welcome him—seemed to throw her into a deeper state of shock, holding her completely still in his arms as she felt her response like a lick of fire burning from mouth to breasts then, worse, to the very core of her sex. Her muscles contracted fiercely in reaction, her lips quivering on yet another helpless gasp.

Then, thankfully, she was free—thankfully because in all her life she had never experienced a response like that! And the fact that she had done so with this perfect stranger both frightened and bewildered her.

'Right,' he muttered. 'Let's get the hell out of here.'

Crazily she found herself leaning weakly against him, sponge-kneed and dizzy with the strange cacophony of reactions taking place inside her. Her mouth was throbbing, her heart trembling and her damp breasts quivering where they were being pressed tightly against his chest.

Inside she was fainting—it was the only way her muzzy head could think of describing that odd, dragging feeling that seemed to be trying to sink her like liquid to the ground. Even the roots of her hair reacted stingingly as his chin brushed across the top of her head when he moved to glance around them.

He shifted her beneath the crook of his powerful arm, and he was big—big enough to fit her easily beneath his shoulder, even though she was no small thing herself. Her hand slid from the long lock of his hair to flutter delicately down his back to his lean, tight waist, her other pressing against the front of his white dress shirt where she was made forcefully aware of the accelerated pounding of his heart beneath the sticky dampness where her wetness had transferred itself to him.

The whole scene must have looked powerfully emotional to anyone watching all of this take place— the notorious Annie Lacey meeting, throwing herself upon and leaving hurriedly with a man who could only be an old and very intimate friend by the way he held her clasped so possessively to him. But, huddled against him as she was, at that moment she could only be glad of his powerful bulk because it helped to hide what had happened to her from all those curious eyes.

But when she felt the cooling freshness of the summer night air hit her body she at last made an effort to pull her befuddled brain together.

'Wait a minute!' she gasped, pulling to a dead stop in front of the row of waiting black cabs. 'I—'

'Just get in,' he instructed, transferring his grip to her elbow and quite forcefully propelling her inside the nearest cab.

Annie landed with less than her usual grace on the cheap, cracked leather seat.

'What the hell do you think you're doing?' she exclaimed with shrill indignity as he climbed right in behind her.

He didn't bother to answer, but instead, and to her horror, began stripping off his black silk evening jacket!

Annie made an ungainly scramble into the furthest corner of the seat, blue eyes revealing the real alarm she was now beginning to feel.

'Where to, mate?'

'Tell the guy,' the man beside her commanded. 'Then put that on—' the jacket landed on her trembling lap '—before his eyes pop out of his head.'

Annie glanced sharply at the cabby to find his eyes fixed on her breasts so shockingly outlined against the sodden fabric of her dress. Dark heat stung along her cheeks as hurriedly she dragged the jacket around her slender shoulders and clutched possessively at its black satin lapels.

'Your address,' her accoster prompted, after having watched sardonically her rush to cover herself up.

Annie flashed him a fulminating look, frustratedly aware that she had no choice but to comply. Well, she did have a choice, she acknowledged bitterly. She could toss this alarming man back his jacket, climb out of the cab and walk back into the hotel to face all those eagerly speculative eyes while she went in search of Todd.

But the very idea of doing that made her feel slightly sick. All those eyes with their amused, knowing looks, and sly sniggers from people who would see the whole thing as yet another Annie Lacey sensation.

Reluctantly she muttered her address, then subsided stiffly into her corner of the cab while he leaned forward to repeat it to the cabby.

Annie followed the lithe movement of his long body with her eyes.

Who is he? she wondered tensely. Though he sounded American there was an added hint of a foreign accent in his deep, gravelly voice that she couldn't quite place. And his skin wore a rich, smooth olive tint that suggested foreign climes—like the colour of his raven-black hair with its outrageous pony-tail lying smoothly along the pure silk of his bright white dress shirt between well-muscled shoulderblades.

What is he? Even in profile his face showed a hard-boned toughness of character that somehow did not go with the flamboyant style of his hair.

He gave a conflict of impressions, she realised, and wondered if it was a deliberately erected façade aimed to put people off the track where his true personality was concerned.

And why did she think that? Because she did it herself and therefore could recognise the same trait in others.

Instruction to the cabby completed, he slid the partitioning window shut then sat back to look at her.

Instantly those strange sparks of awareness prickled along the surface of her skin—an awareness of his firm, sculptured mouth that had so shockingly claimed her own, of lips that made hers tingle in memory, made her throat go dry as they stretched into a smooth, mocking smile.

'A novel way of meeting, don't you think?' he drawled.

Not gravel but velvet. She found herself correcting her description of the liquid tones of his voice. And laced with a hint of—what? Contempt? Sarcasm? Or just simple, wry amusement at the whole situation? Annie flicked her wary glance up to his eyes. Strange eyes. Green. Green eyes that again did not go with the dark Latin rest of him, and were certainly alight with something that kept her senses alert to the threat of danger.

Danger?

'You were watching me earlier,' she said half-accusingly. 'And you know my name.'

He smiled at that, the wry—yes, it was wry—amusement deepening in his eyes. 'But you are a very beautiful woman, Miss Lacey,' he pointed out. 'Your face and your body can be seen plastered on billboards all over the world. Of course I know your name.' He gave a small shrug of those wide, white-clad shoulders. 'I would expect every red-blooded man alive to recognise you on sight.'

'Except that all those other men do not make a point of stalking me all evening,' she pointed out.

His attention sharpened. 'Are you by any chance trying to imply something specific?' he enquired carefully.

Was she? She was by nature very suspicious of men in general. This one seemed to have gone out of his way to be where he was right now.

'Perhaps you suspect me of spilling the champagne deliberately?' he suggested, when Annie did not say anything.

'Did you?' Cool blue eyes threw back a challenge.

He smiled—the kind of noncommittal smile that tried to mock her for even thinking such a thing about him. But she was not convinced by it, or put off.

'Things like it have happened before,' she told him. 'In my business you collect nut cases like other people collect postage stamps.'

'And you see me as the ideal candidate for that kind of weird behaviour?' He looked so amused by the idea that it made her angry.

'You can't tell by just looking at them, you know,' she snapped. 'They don't have "crazy man" stamped on their foreheads to give me a clue.'

'But in your business, Miss Lacey, you must surely accept that kind of thing as merely par for the course.'

'And therefore relinquish the right to care?'

He offered no answer to that, but his eyes narrowed thoughtfully on her as though he was making a quick reassessment of something he had already set in his mind about her, and a small silence fell.

Annie turned her head away to stare out the cab window so that she did not have to try and read what that reassessment was about. Why, she wasn't sure, except . . .

She sighed inwardly. She knew why. She'd looked away because he disturbed her oddly. His dark good looks disturbed her. The way he had been staring at her earlier disturbed her. His shocking kisses had disturbed her, awakening feelings inside her that she had honestly believed she did not possess.

The black cab rumbled on, stopping and starting in London's busy night traffic. People were out in force, the warm summer night and the fact that it was tourist season in the city filling the streets with life. Pub doors stood wedged open to help ease the heated air inside rooms packed with casually dressed, enviably relaxed people. Cafés with their pavements blocked continental-style by white plastic tables had busy waiters running to and fro, and the sights and smells and sounds were those of a busy international metropolis, all shapes, sizes, colours and creeds mingling in a mad, warm bustle of easy harmony.

She sighed softly to herself, wishing that she could be like them, wishing that she could walk out and mingle inconspicuously with the crowd and just soak up some of that carefree atmosphere. But she couldn't. Her looks were her fortune, and therefore were too well-known—as the man sitting beside her had just pointed out. Dressed in jeans and a T-shirt with a scarf covering her head, she would still be recognised. She knew because she'd tried it.

The trouble was, she decided heavily, she was becoming weary of the life she led, the restrictions that life placed on her. Tired of an image that she had created for herself which meant her always having to be on her guard with people—people like the man sitting beside her.

'The champagne caught your hair.' The sudden touch of light fingers on a sticky tendril of hair just by her left ear had Annie reacting instinctively.

She jerked violently away from his touch. He went very still, his strange eyes narrowing on her face with an expression that she found difficult to define as he slowly lowered his hand again, long, blunt-ended fingers settling lightly on his own lap.

A new silence began to fizz between them, and Annie did not know what to say to break it. There was something about this man that frightened her—no matter how much she tried to tell herself that she was being paranoid about him. Even that touch—that light, innocent brush of his fingers against her hair—had filled her with the most incredible alarm. Her heart was hammering too, rattling against her ribs with enough force to restrict her breathing.

She bit down on her lower lip, even white teeth pressing into lush, ruby-coloured flesh, and her dusky lashes lowered to hide her discomfort as warm colour began to seep into her cheeks.

Then the cab made a sharp turn, and she saw with relief that they were turning into a narrow cobbled street of pretty, whitewashed cottages, one of which was her own.

Almost eagerly she shifted towards the edge of the seat so that she could jump out just as soon as they stopped. The sound of soft laughter beside her made her throw a wary glance at her companion.

He was smiling, ruefully shaking his sleek dark head.
'I am not intending to jump on you, you know,' he
drawled. 'I assure you I do possess a little more finesse
than to seduce my women in the back seats of black
cabs. And,' he went on, before Annie could think of a
thing to say in reply, 'I did think my behaviour exemplary
enough to give me gallant-knight status if nothing else.'

He thought those kisses in the hotel foyer exemplary
behaviour? She didn't. And he could sit there smiling
that innocently mocking smile as long as he wanted to,
but she would not lower her guard to him. Her senses
were just too alert to the hidden danger in him to do
that.

'I'm sorry,' she said coolly. 'But gallant knights are
so few and far between that a girl does not expect to
meet one these days.'

The taxi came to a stop outside her tiny mews cottage
then—thankfully. Because she was suddenly very des-
perate to get away from this strange, disturbing man.

But as she went to slip off his jacket and opened her
mouth to utter some polite little word of thanks for his
trouble he stopped her.

'No.' His hand descended onto her shoulder to hold
his jacket in place. 'Keep it until we arrive at your door,'
he quietly advised, sending a pointed glance at the cab
driver. 'One can only imagine what the champagne has
done to the fabric of your dress by now.'

She went pale, remembering that awful moment when
she'd caught the cab driver's gaze fixed on her breasts,
so transparently etched against her sodden dress.

'Thank you,' she whispered, clutching the jacket back
around her.

He said nothing, opening the taxi door and stepping
out, then turning to help her join him before he bent to
pass some money through the driver's open window.
Annie supposed that she should offer to pay the fare,

but somehow this man gave the impression that he would not appreciate such egalitarian gestures. There was an air of the old-fashioned autocrat about him—an indomitable pride in the set of those wide shoulders flexing beneath the white dress shirt as he straightened and turned back to face her.

She shuddered, feeling oddly as though something or someone had just walked over her grave.

'Y-you should have held the taxi,' she murmured stiffly as the black cab rumbled off down the street, belching out pungent diesel fumes as it went.

If he picked up on her unspoken warning—that if he was standing in the belief that she was going to invite him into her home then he was mistaken—he did not show it, merely shrugging those big shoulders dismissively as he turned towards her black-painted front door.

'Your key?' he prompted.

Disconcerted by his calm indifference to any hint she had given him, she decided grimly not to argue, lowering her pale head to watch her fingers fumble nervously with the tiny catch on her soft gold leather evening bag to get at the key. The quicker she got the door open, the sooner she could get rid of him, she decided, wondering crossly what the heck was the matter with her. She didn't usually feel like this.

She didn't usually get herself into crazy situations like this one either. She was very careful not to do so normally.

Normal. What was normal about any of this?

Refusing to allow her fingers to tremble, she fitted the key into the lock, pushed open the door, then forced herself back around to face him. 'Thank you,' she said firmly, 'for bringing me home. And—' she allowed him a small, dry smile '—for saving my embarrassment.'

'Think nothing of it.' He sent her a little bow that was pure, old-fashioned gallantry and befitted somehow this

tall dark man who reminded her so much of a throwback
from another age. South American, maybe? she wondered curiously, then shuddered, not wanting him to be.
She had a strange, unexplainable suspicion that it would
actually hurt her to find that he might be the same
nationality as Alvarez.

If he was aware of her curiosity he did not offer to
relieve it. Instead, and with another one of those bows,
he held his hand out towards her as though he were going
to grab hold and push her into the house.

Defensively she took a big step back, bringing herself
hard up against the white-painted stone wall behind her,
and almost choking on an uplift of clamouring fear.

'My jacket,' he reminded her softly.

Oh, God. Annie closed her eyes, angry with herself
because she knew that she was behaving like an idiot and
really had no reason for it. He had, as he had pointed
out, shown her exemplary behaviour over the whole
messy incident!

Except for those kisses, she reminded herself tensely.
Those kisses had not been exemplary at all.

Lips pressed tightly together over her clenched teeth,
she slipped off the jacket and handed it to him. 'Thank
you,' she murmured without looking at him.

'My pleasure,' he drawled, his long fingers sliding
delicately over hers as he took the jacket from her. Her
own began to tingle, fine, sharp showers of sensation
skittering across the surface of her skin to make her
tremble as she whipped her arm across her body in an
effort to hide herself from those terribly disturbing eyes.

Casually he hooked a finger through the loop and
draped the jacket over his shoulder, his lazy stance
showing no signs that he was going to go away.

Annie waited, praying fiercely that he was not standing
here expecting her to invite him in. No man other than
Todd had ever stepped a single foot inside her home.

And only Todd had done so because he had proved time and time again that she could trust him with her very life.

She thought of this house as her sanctuary—the only place where she felt she could relax and truly be herself. She didn't want to give way to the compelling urge he seemed to be silently pressing on her to break that rule and invite him to enter.

Panic began to bubble up from the anxious pit of her stomach—panic at the man's indomitable refusal to be brushed off by her, and panic at the knowledge that if he kept this small, silent battle up she was going to be the one to give in.

Then he touched her.

And, good grief, everything vital inside her went haywire—muscles, nerves, senses, heart, all clamouring out of control as his hand cupped gently at her chin, lifted it, forcing her wary blue gaze to meet the probing expression in his.

He didn't say anything, but a frown marred that high, satin-smooth brow as though he was reassessing—again—and was still not sure what he was seeing when he looked at the infamous Annie Lacey.

'Beautiful,' he murmured almost to himself, then bent suddenly, blocking out the dim lamplight as his mouth swooped down to press a soft, light kiss to her trembling mouth. 'More than beautiful,' he extended as he straightened again. 'Dangerous.' Then he said, 'Goodnight, Miss Lacey,' and simply turned and walked away, leaving her standing there staring at his long, loose, easy stride with his jacket thrown over one broad shoulder while that shocking pelt of raven hair rested comfortably along his straight spine.

And she felt strangely at odds with herself—as though she had just let go of something potentially very important to her and had no way of snatching it back.

# CHAPTER THREE

IT WAS crazy, she told herself later as she pulled a smooth satin robe over her freshly showered body.

It had been a crazy night with a crazy end that had left her with this crazy sense of deep disappointment that she couldn't seem to shake off.

What's the matter with you? she asked herself impatiently. You should be feeling relieved, not disappointed that he didn't take advantage of a situation most men would have leapt at if they'd found Annie Lacey beholden to them for something!

Or maybe, she then found herself thinking, it was *because* she was the notorious Annie Lacey that he had not taken advantage. Perhaps he was the kind of man who did not involve himself with the Annie Laceys of this world.

Perhaps, for once, your reputation has worked against you.

What?

No.

'That's sick thinking, Annie,' she muttered to herself.

And anyway, you cannot be feeling annoyed about a lost opportunity you had no intention of taking up yourself!

Remember Luis Alvarez, she told herself grimly. Remembering him was enough to put any woman off all those dark Latin types for good!

With that levelling reminder, she tightened her robe's belt around her waist and flounced out of the bedroom, aware that there was more than a little defiance in the way she slammed the door shut on the thoughts she had left on the other side.

Her house was not big, really nothing more than an old-fashioned terraced cottage renovated to modern-day standards. The upper floor housed her one bedroom, which had been carefully fitted to utilise minimum space for maximum storage, and a rather decadent bathroom, with its spa bath and pulse-action shower that could massage the aches out of the worst day's modelling. The stairway dropped directly into her small sitting room-cum-dining room, where the clever use of lighting and pastel shades made it a pleasure to her eye each time she entered.

The kitchen was a super-efficient blend of modern appliances and limed oak. Annie padded across the cool ceramic floor to fill the kettle for a cup of good, strong tea.

The best panacea to cure all ills, she told herself bracingly. Even the ills of a silly woman in conflict with no one but herself!

Crazy. Crazy, crazy, she sighed to herself as she leant against a unit to gaze out on the dark night while she waited for the kettle to boil.

Most of her life had been lived in busy high profile. Her ability to act and her photogenic looks had been picked up on and used from a very early age. While Aunt Claire had been alive she had been buffered from most of the flak that went with a well-known face by a woman who had been fiercely protective of Annie's privacy. But after her aunt had died and with what came afterwards Annie had suddenly found herself the constant cynosure of all eyes.

Which was why she loved her little house so much. She loved the sense of well-being and security that it always filled her with to be shut alone inside it. It was here and only here that she felt able to relax enough to drop her guard and be herself—though, she then thought, she was not really sure she knew who or what that person was, having never really been given the time or chance to find out.

Was it that sombre-faced person she could see staring back at her in the darkened reflection of the kitchen window? she wondered. She hoped not. Those eyes looked just a little too lost and lonely for her peace of mind, and her mouth had a vulnerable tilt to it that unsettled her slightly because she did not consider herself vulnerable to anything much—except contempt, she conceded. Others' contempt of her could still cut and cut deeply.

As could rejection, she added. Or—to be more precise—cold rejection, usually administered by women who felt threatened by her, but sometimes by men. Men of that stranger's calibre. Cool, self-possessed, autocratic men who—

She pulled herself up short, a frown marring the smooth brow she could see in the window. Now why had her mind skipped back to him again? He had not held her in contempt—or if he had he had not shown it. Nor had he rejected her—not in the ice-cold way she'd been musing about just then.

He was a stranger—just a mere, passing stranger who had helped her out of an embarrassing spot then quietly gone on his way, that was all.

The trouble with you, Annie Lacey, she told herself grimly, is that you've become so damned cynical about the opposite sex that you actually expect every one of them to take advantage of you whenever they possibly can!

And could it be that you're feeling just a teeny bit miffed because he did *not* take advantage of the situation?

I wish . . .

And just what do you wish? that more sensible side of her brain derided. For a nice, ordinary man to come along to sweep you off your dainty feet and take you away from all of this? Two things wrong with that wish, Annie. One—you made this particular bed you are now lying so uncomfortably on. And two—that man was no ordinary man. He was strong, dark and excitingly mysterious.

And you fancied him like hell, she finally admitted. But he obviously did not fancy you!

And that's what you're feeling so miffed about!

She grimaced at that, and was glad that the kettle decided to boil at that moment so that she could switch her thoughts to other things.

She was just pouring tea into her cup when the telephone began to ring.

Todd, she decided. It had to be. He would be ringing up to find out just what had happened to her, and a rueful smile was curving her mouth as she took her cup of tea with her into her sitting room and dropped into the corner of a soft-cushioned sofa before lifting the receiver to her ear.

'What the hell happened to you?' It was Todd, sounding angry and anxious all at the same time, God bless him. 'One minute you were off to the loo, the next I'm being informed that you were seen in a mad, passionate clinch with some guy, then disappearing out of the door with him! Who the hell is he? And what the hell were you doing just walking out on me like that?'

She shifted uncomfortably, taking her time curling her bare toes beneath her while she tried to decide how to answer all of that. There was no way she was going to admit the truth, that was for sure. it was bad enough knowing what a fool she'd been, getting into a taxi with a complete stranger, but telling Todd of all people that not only had she done exactly that but she'd also let the stranger kiss her in front of half of London's best would make him think that she'd gone temporarily insane!

Crazy. The whole thing was crazy.

'Oh, just an old friend from way back,' she heard herself say lightly. 'And we weren't kissing,' she lied. 'We were plotting because some stupid fool had spilled a full glass of champagne down my front, and you don't need much imagination to know what that must have done to my dress.'

'God, yes!' he gasped, obviously not lacking the imagination needed to guess what the skimpy silk would have looked like wet. 'Are you all right? Why didn't you come and get me? Is he still there with you now?'

Annie had to smile at the quick-fired set of questions. 'I'm fine,' she replied. 'I didn't come and get you because quite frankly, darling, I was not in a fit state to go anywhere but straight home. And no, he is not still here.'

'You said an old friend,' he murmured thoughtfully. 'I didn't know you had any male friends but me.'

'Well, there's conceit for you,' she drawled, thinking, He's right, I don't. And she felt suddenly very empty inside.

'Who?' Todd demanded. 'What's his name?'

'No one you know,' she dismissed, realising with a start that she hadn't even bothered to ask his name!

Crazy. You really are going crazy, Annie!

'A male model,' she said, forcing her mind back to Todd's question. 'I met him on that promo I did for Cable last year. Who told you I was kissing him?' she demanded with commendable affront, to throw him off the track.

There was a short pause before his deriding, 'Guess,' came down the line at her.

'Susie,' she sighed. She should have known.

'She took great delight in telling me how she'd seen you lost in a heated clinch with another man before you walked off and left me,' he related grimly. 'Then had the bloody gall to suggest I see her home instead!'

'To which you replied?' she prompted.

'Guess again, darling,' he drawled. 'I'm still here at this wretched mêlée if that gives you a clue.'

Yes, it gave her a big clue, and Annie's heart ached for him.

'If she thought she could walk up to me and start slandering you in one breath then expect me to fall back into her arms in the next then she soon learned otherwise,' he went on tightly. 'She eventually left with that guy from the Rouez Sands Group.'

'And made sure you saw her leave with him, of course.'

'Oh, yes,' he sighed.

'You OK?' she asked him gently.

'No,' he said. 'But I'll live.'

Annie smothered a sigh, wishing that she could ease the pain she knew he was suffering right now. But only Susie could do that, and the foolish woman was too jealous of Annie to see that by blackening Annie to Todd she was only making things worse for herself.

In all fairness Annie didn't completely blame Susie for being suspicious about their relationship. It did look suspicious to anyone looking in on it. But even though she'd urged Todd often enough to tell Susie the truth he'd refused, going all stiff and adamant in a way that told her that Susie's suspicions offended his pride. 'It cuts both ways,' was all he ever said. 'If she can't trust my word that there is nothing intimate between you and me, then why should I trust her with the full truth about us?'

Stalemate, and likely to stay that way while both of them remained so pig-headed about it all.

'Give me a call soon,' he murmured as a conclusion to the conversation, then added as an afterthought, 'But not during the rest of this week, because I'll be in Madrid trying to whip up that extra injection of cash I need to secure *Cliché* Europe's safe launch.'

Annie frowned, having forgotten all about that. Todd had told her about it only this evening—the surprising and worrying fact that he was taking a big risk publishing a new glossy in the present economic climate. 'The trouble is,' he'd explained ruefully, 'I stagnate if I don't and stand to lose everything if I do.'

'What I need,' he murmured thoughtfully now, 'is something really exclusive to front the first issue— something that will guarantee sales and therefore appeal to my backers. I just haven't come up with what that exclusive something is yet.'

'You will,' she stated, with soft confidence in his ability. 'And if all else fails I could always pose nude,' she suggested. 'That'll be a world first and guarantee you a complete sell-out.'

'You'd do it too, wouldn't you?' he murmured curiously, hearing the note of seriousness threading through her lighter tone.

'For you?' she said. 'I would sell my very soul for you, my darling, and that's the truth. But I would much rather not,' she then added. 'So try to come up with something less—sensational for me, will you?' she pleaded.

'I promise,' he laughed. 'Not that the idea of you posing nude does not appeal,' he teased. 'But I think I should be able to come up with something more—subtle. So take care, and be good while I'm away.'

When am I ever anything else? Annie thought as she replaced the receiver and grimaced at the dark sense of dissatisfaction that began niggling at her nerves.

And all because a stranger managed to get beneath that protective skin you wear? she mocked herself.

'Goodness me, Annie,' she muttered aloud, and then thought, You must be feeling starved of affection to have one small incident affect you as much as you're allowing this to do.

Bed, she decided. Bed before you become even more maudlin than you already are!

But she didn't sleep well, her dreams seeming haunted by a tall dark figure who kept insisting on kissing her, his warm mouth constantly closing over her own every time she tried to speak! But, worse than that, she didn't try to fight him but always, always welcomed him— helplessly, eagerly! Then she ended up waking in a breathless state of shock at her own wanton imagination.

It was terrible. She was ashamed of herself! 'Sex-starved, that's what you are,' she muttered, and gave her pillow an angry thump before settling down to experience the self-same dream all over again!

Consequently she was not in a very good frame of mind when her phone began ringing at what felt like the break of dawn that morning.

Grumbling incoherently to herself, she tried to ignore it at first, stuffing her head beneath her pillow and pretending the noise was not there. But it didn't stop, and after a while she sighed, sat up, rubbed at her gritty eyes then reached out with a lazy hand to lift the receiver.

'Annie!' Lissa's excited voice hit her eardrums like the clash from a hundred cymbals. 'Get our neat botty out of that bed! *Cliché*'s got its launch. And we have one hell of a panic on!'

A panic. She would call it more than a panic, Annie decided grumpily as she dragged herself to the transit lounge at Barbados's Grantley Adams airport over twelve hours later.

'But I'm due in Paris on Tuesday!' she'd exclaimed in protest when Lissa had finished giving her the hurried details of Todd's great coup.

'All changed, darling,' her agent had said. 'Everything cancelled for the next two weeks in favour of this.'

'This' being Todd's brainwave—which had apparently hit him after he had been talking to her on the phone last night.

Or—to be more precise—someone else had hit him with it.

The great and glorious Adamas, no less.

And, even despite not wanting to be, Annie was impressed.

Adamas jewellery was the most expensive anyone could buy. The man who worked under that trade name was a legend because he designed and produced every single breathtakingly exquisite piece himself, using only the finest stones and setting them in precious metal. All the world's richest women clamoured to possess them.

He was a genius in his field. His last collection had taken five years to put together, and had sold out in five minutes. That must have been—Annie frowned, trying to remember—four years ago at least.

And late last night, it seemed, Todd had found himself talking to none other than Adamas himself! He hadn't known, of course, whom he was sharing a nightcap with. Hardly anyone alive on this earth knew who the real Adamas actually was, because the man was some kind of eccentric recluse!

But, according to Lissa, during this chat over a drink Todd's journalistic mind must have been alerted by something Adamas had said, and he'd begun to suspect just whom he was drinking with. So he had gone for it—asked the man outright—and, lo and behold, found out that he was right!

One thing had led to another, and a few drinks later Todd had discovered that the guy had just completed his latest collection. And that had been when his brainstorm had hit. A blind shot, he'd called it. He'd suggested what a coup it would be if *Cliché* launched with Annie Lacey wearing the latest Adamas collection. And to his surprise the great man had agreed!

And that, neatly put, was why Annie had just spent the last twelve hours travelling.

Adamas had agreed, but only on his own strict terms—one being that the whole thing had to take place immediately or not at all, another that he chose the location and—something insisted on because of the priceless value of the subject matter in hand—that the whole thing must be carried out in the utmost secrecy!

Which was also why she was now stuck in transit, waiting to find out what the rest of her travel arrangements were. Lissa had only been privy to Annie's travel plan this far. The rest was to be revealed.

But that would not be before she'd had a chance to change out of the faded jeans and baggy old sweatshirt that had been part of her disguise along with a sixties floppy velvet hat into which she'd had her hair stuffed for the last twelve hours to comply with his demand for secrecy, she decided grimly.

She was hot, she was tired, and she felt grubby. And, grabbing her flight bag, she made her way to the ladies' room, deciding that any further travelling could wait until she felt more comfortable.

Half an hour later, and dressed more appropriately for the Caribbean in a soft white Indian cotton skirt and matching blouse, with her hair scooped into a high topknot, she was being ushered out into the burning sun and across the tarmac towards a twin engined, eight-seater aeroplane which was to take her to Union Island, the gateway to the Grenadines, or so she'd been informed by the attendant who'd come to collect her.

An hour after that she found herself standing in the shimmering heat of her third airport of the day, where a beautiful young woman with perfect brown skin and a gentle smile was trying to usher her towards a waiting helicopter!

'But where am I supposed to be going to?' she demanded irritably, growing tired of all this cloak-and-dagger stuff.

'To one of our beautiful smaller islands, privately leased from our government by your host,' the young woman informed her smoothly, and strode off in the wake of Annie's luggage, which was being carried by an airport lackey.

'Host,' she muttered tetchily. Did anyone know the actual name of the great Adamas? Or did his desire for privacy mean that even his name was a carefully guarded secret?

Her luggage had been stowed by the time she reached the helicopter, its lethal blades already rotating impatiently. She was instructed to duck her head a little as she ran beneath them, then was helped to clamber in beside the pilot.

With a smile and a gesture of farewell the young woman closed the door, and the sudden change from deafening noise to near silence was a shock. Annie straightened in her seat, smoothed down the soft folds of her skirt, blinked a couple of times in an effort to clear her bewildered head, then turned to look at the pilot.

And almost fainted in surprise.

Long black hair, tied back at the tanned nape by a thin black strip of ribbon, lean dark face with green eyes smiling sardonically at her.

It was her rescuer from the night before.

And the man she had let seduce her all night long in her dreams.

'You!' she gasped, feeling an upsurge of guilty heat burn her insides when her eyes automatically dropped to his shockingly familiar mouth.

'Good afternoon, Miss Lacey,' he drawled, enjoying the reaction he was having on her.

'But—what are you doing here?'

'Why, I live here,' he smoothly replied, and touched something that sent a burst of power into the engines. 'Please fasten yourself in; we are about to take off.'

'But...' She couldn't move for the shock of it. 'You're a helicopter pilot?' she choked out eventually.

'Among other things.' He smiled, humour leaping to that magnetically attractive mouth at what, Annie realised almost as soon as she'd said it, was about the most stupid thing she had ever said. 'Your belt,' he prompted. 'We will talk later.'

Then he was flicking the headset he had resting around his neck up over his ears and dismissing her as he turned his attention to the task in hand, leaving her to fumble numbly with her belt while he spoke smoothly to air-traffic control. Then, without warning, they were up in the air.

Annie gasped at the unexpectedness of it, staring with wide eyes as the ground simply dropped away beneath them. Her heart leapt into her mouth, her lungs refused to function, and, of course, the slight numbing effect of jet lag was not helping her discern what the heck was going on here.

They paused, hovering like a hawk about to swoop, then shot forwards in a way that threw her back into her seat. He glanced at her sharply, then away again, a small smile playing about his lips which seemed to err more towards satisfaction than anything else.

Then suddenly she was covering her eyes as they seemed to shoot directly towards the bright orange ball of sun hanging low in the sky.

Something dropped on her lap. Peering down, she saw a pair of gold-rimmed sunglasses and gratefully pushed them on. Able to see again without suffering for it, she turned to look curiously at him.

He too had donned a pair of sunglasses; gold-rimmed like her own pair, they sat neatly across the bridge of his long, thin nose, seeming to add a certain pizzazz to an already rivetingly attractive face.

Last time she'd seen him he had been standing at her front door wearing a severely conventional black dinner suit and bow-tie. He had seemed alarmingly daunting to her fanciful mind then.

Now those same sparks of alarm came back to worry her, darting across her skin, because here in this contraption, with the full blast of the Caribbean sun shining on his face, he had taken on a far more dangerously appealing appearance. His skin looked richer, his features more keenly etched. The thin cream shirt he was wearing was tucked into the pleated waist of a pair of wheat-coloured linen slacks, offering a more casual view of him that made her want to back off even while she was drawn towards it.

'Why are you here?' she asked as her nerves began to steady. 'Or—' she then clarified that '—why am I here with you?'

'You do not know?' He flicked her a glance before returning his attention to what he was doing, but the look had been enough to make her stupid mind click into action, and she sat there staring at him in utter disbelief.

'You—are Adamas?' she gasped.

He didn't answer—didn't need to. It was written in that small smile that touched briefly at the corner of his mouth. 'We are going to my island,' he informed her smoothly instead. 'It sits just beyond the main string of islands, lapped by the Caribbean on one side and the Atlantic on the other...'

Annie was barely listening; she was still staring unblinkingly at him, trying to fit her impression of what the Adamas man should look like to the one he actually was!

An eccentric recluse? This—Adonis of a man with more muscle than fat and an air about him that still made her think more of the Spanish Inquisition than an artistic genius. Blinking, she found herself staring at his hands—long hands, strong hands with the signs of manual labour scored into the supple palms, long fingers, blunt-ended, with neatly shorn nails. The hands of a man who worked fine metal into those intricate designs that she had been privileged to glimpse once around the neck of a very wealthy woman?

'I don't believe it,' she muttered, more to herself than to him.

But he shrugged carelessly, as if her opinion did not bother him. 'I am what I am, Miss Lacey,' he drawled indifferently. Then almost too casually he went on, 'As you are what you undoubtedly are.'

An insult—Annie didn't even try to mistake it for anything but what it was. But before she could challenge him about it again they veered sharply to one side, sending her heart leaping into her mouth again when she found herself staring sideways out of the helicopter onto a half-moon stretch of glistening silver sand.

'My home,' he announced. 'Or one of them,' he then added coolly. 'The island is a quarter of a mile wide and half a mile long. It has a shape like a hooked nose which is where it gets its name—Hook-nose Island. My villa sits in the hook—see?'

Dipping the helicopter, he swooped down towards the island, bringing the two-storey white plantation-style house swinging dizzyingly up towards them. Then, before she had time to catch her breath at that little bit of showmanship, he levelled the helicopter off and hovered so that she could focus on the palm-tree-lined lawns that swept down from the house to the silver beach she had seen first.

'Hook-nose Bay is a bathers' paradise,' he said. 'The natural curve of the land itself and the coral reef at the bay's mouth protect it from the worst of the weather and any unwelcome aquatic visitors with sharp teeth.'

'Sharks?' she asked nervously.

He nodded. 'These islands are famous for their resident Nurse Sharks. But it is safe to bathe there in the bay—though the rest of the island is not so safe,' he warned. 'Strong currents and sometimes angry seas can make bathing on any of the other little coves you see quite dangerous. Especially on the Atlantic side.'

As he turned them neatly to face in the opposite direction Annie gazed curiously down to where a thick tropical wood clustered around a hump in the centre of the island, at the bottom of which the house nestled against its lushly carpeted slope. On the other side of the hill sheer drops of craggy rock fell abruptly downwards to jagged inlets where the Atlantic tossed itself against them in foaming white crests.

This side of the little island was a stark contrast to the other softer, more gentle side that the house faced. It would be an unlucky sailor who came upon this island from that direction, she noted with a small shudder.

Then she gasped as they began to drop like a stone towards the ground. They landed gently, though, her sigh of relief bringing a mocking look from the man beside her before he turned his attention to shutting down the engine and going through some kind of mental check-list before he opened his door and jumped out.

He came around to help her, having to stoop low beneath the slowing blades and warning her to do the same as his hands circled her slender waist to assist her. Then they were running free, both bent almost double, Annie with a hand covering her eyes to stop the whirls of dust from blowing into them.

Pulling to a halt about ten yards away from the helicopter, he turned to watch as she dusted down her clothes with her hands. They'd landed on a natural plateau of rock not far away from the house. But, sand being sand, it had found its way up here, blown probably by the trade winds that acted like natural air-conditioning to most of these islands.

'Come,' he said when she'd concluded her tidy-up by brushing light fingertips over her hair and cheeks. 'I will bring your luggage later. But now you must be in dire need of a drink.'

She was and didn't demur, following him across a neatly kept lawn and up the few steps which took them into the lower veranda's shade.

The two solid wood front doors stood open in welcome. He led the way into a deliciously cool entrance hall, where Annie paused to catch her breath and study with still slightly bewildered eyes the blatant luxury of Aubusson thrown down on top of richly polished wood.

For a mere hallway it was huge—as big as any other room in a house of this size. 'Grand' was the word that slid into her mind. Old masters with a nautical theme hung in heavy gold frames on plain, white-painted walls and a great staircase swept up from its central location to a galleried landing that seemed to form a circle around the whole upper floor.

A woman appeared from the back of the house. Short, thin and wiry, with greying hair swept away from a severe face, she was wearing all black. She greeted her employer with some words in what Annie half-recognised as Spanish, to which he replied in the same language, his voice seeming to grow more liquid, more sensually disturbing to Annie's agitated mind.

'Margarita,' he informed Annie, watching as the two women exchanged shy, slightly stiff smiles. 'Between them, she and her husband Pedro take care of everything here. If you will please come this way—' he held out an arm in invitation '—Margarita will bring us some refreshment.'

As the woman bustled off towards the back of the house Annie followed her host across the hall and into a large, bright, sunny room with full-length French-style windows standing open to the gentle sea breeze.

Momentarily diverted, she moved over to look at the view, and stood transfixed by what she saw. Before her lay a dramatic mix of lush green lawns rolling down towards a crescent of silver sand, followed by the pale aquamarine shades of shallow waters deepening to rich gentian-blue. Several beautiful flame-trees with their branches laden with vivid red blooms were scattered around the grounds. The sun was hanging low—a deep golden globe shimmering in a melting turquoise sky.

And when she heard movement behind her she turned an enraptured smile to the man she found propped up against the closed door, mockery and arrogance in every line of his body as he stood there with one neat ankle crossed over the other, arms folded across his big chest.

'Well, well,' he drawled. 'So the notorious Miss Lacey can still experience a childlike enchantment at something beautiful and unspoiled. Who would have thought it?'

Annie went still, her smile dying as she was suddenly assailed by a cold, dark sense of menace, his lazy masculine stance, his insolent expression and his deriding words all helping to remind her of something that she should have never let herself forget. Men were the enemy. And this particular man was no different.

'Who are you?' she demanded quietly.

'Who am I?' he repeated, the mockery hard and spiked. 'Why, I am Adamas,' he informed her lazily. 'Loosely translated, it means diamond-hard—impenetrable. But in this case we shall call me a—rock,' he decided. 'A rock on which you, Annie Lacey, have just been neatly marooned.'

# CHAPTER FOUR

'MAROONED.' Annie frowned at him, trying to decide whether he was just attempting a very poor joke. But his face held no hint of humour, only a smile that sent the blood running cold through her veins.

Marooned, she repeated silently and slowly to herself. Abandoned. Isolated without resources. He had used the word quite deliberately.

It hit her then that this was no simple commission in which the great Adamas employed the notorious Annie Lacey to promote his priceless gems. She had been brought here under false pretences—brought here and isolated from the rest of the world by this man for some specific purpose of his own.

A sick sense of *déjà vu* washed over her, filling her eyes with unmistakable horror as Luis Alvarez's hot face loomed up in her mind, and for a moment—a small moment—she lost control, face paling, breasts heaving, eyes haunted as they glanced around for somewhere to run.

'Perfect,' he drawled, making her blink at the soft-voiced sensuality that he managed to thread into the one simple word. 'That look of maidenly panic must have taken hours of practice in front of your mirror to cultivate. Allow that gorgeous mouth to quiver just a little,' he suggested, 'and you will be well on the way to convincing me that the well-seasoned vamp is actually a terrified virgin.'

Margarita used that moment to knock on the door. He moved smoothly, loose-limbed and lazily controlled,

51

to open the door and stand aside while his shyly smiling servant wheeled in a trolley laid out with coffee things and some daintily prepared sandwiches.

Annie watched, unable to so much as move a muscle as the other woman murmured in Spanish to her employer and he answered in deep casual replies. The trolley was wheeled over to stand beside a low table between two big, soft-cushioned sofas of a pale coral-pink. Then Margarita was leaving again, murmuring what must have been her thanks to her employer for holding the door for her.

'Who are you really?' Annie demanded once they were alone. 'And will you kindly explain what this—stupid charade is all about?'

'I am who I said I am,' he replied with infuriating blandness. 'I am Adamas. I told you no lies, Miss Lacey.' Moving gracefully, he went over to the trolley then turned a questioning look at her. 'Tea—coffee?' he asked. 'Margarita has prepared both.'

Impatiently Annie shook her head. She wanted nothing in this house until she got some answers. Nothing. 'Is that supposed to make sense to me?' she snapped out impatiently.

'No,' he conceded. 'But then—I never meant to.' A brief smile touched his mouth before he turned his attention to pouring himself a cup of dark, rich coffee. The aroma drifted across the room to torment Annie's parched mouth, forcing her to swallow drily, but other than that she ignored the temptation to change her mind. 'Won't you at least sit down?' he offered politely.

Again she shook her head—for the same reason. 'I just want you to tell me what is going on,' she insisted.

He studied her for a moment, those strange green eyes glinting thoughtfully at her from between glossy black lashes, as if he was considering forcing her to sit and drink.

Whatever, the look had the effect of pushing up her chin, her blue eyes challenging him just to try it and see what he got!

Though what he would get if he did decide to force her physically, she wasn't sure. She was tall, but this man seemed to fill the whole room with his threatening presence. And she couldn't help quailing deep down inside because she knew that if he did call her bluff she would have no choice but to do exactly what he wanted her to do.

And it is that, Annie, she told herself grimly, which keeps you standing as far away from him as you can get! He reminds you of Luis Alvarez—the same height, the same colouring, the same arrogance that made men like them believe that they could say, be and do anything they liked! And if he was Adamas then he also possessed the same money and power in society to have anything nasty about himself that he would not wish the world to hear covered up.

Like the abduction of unwilling females.

She shuddered, unable to control herself. She should have known from the moment she laid eyes on him last night—had known! Her well-tuned instincts had sent out warning signals straight away! But she had let his easy manner lull her into a false sense of security. And, dammit, she'd liked him! Actually allowed herself to like him for the way he had behaved!

She had never been able to say that for Luis, she remembered bitterly. Luis Alvarez had turned her stomach from the moment she'd found herself alone with him. But then, Luis Alvarez had been at least ten years older than this man, his good looks spoiled by ten years' more cynicism and dissolution.

This man did not turn her stomach in that same way, she realised worriedly. And maybe that was one of the reasons why he frightened her perhaps more than Alvarez had ever done. He frightened her because she was reluctantly attracted to him. His calculating study of her frightened her. His softly spoken words that held so many hidden messages frightened her. But, above all, the actual air she was breathing was frightening her—simply because it was filled with the appealing scent of him.

Did he know it? she wondered anxiously. Could he tell what kind of effect he was having on her? His eyes were burning over her—burning in a way that told her that, whatever else was going on here, he too liked what he saw.

The air thickened, became impossible to breathe as the silence between them grew hot and heavy. Then, without warning, he looked down and away.

It was like having something vital taken from her, and Annie had to measure carefully the air she dragged into her suddenly gasping lungs in case she should hyperventilate.

'OK,' he conceded coolly. 'We talk.'

He brought those green eyes to hers again, and there was something overwhelmingly proud in the way his chin lifted along with the eyes.

'My name,' he announced, 'is César DeSanquez. Adamas is merely a name under which I trade...'

DeSanquez, DeSanquez, Annie was thinking frowningly. The name rang a rather cold bell inside her head. It was a name that evoked an image of great wealth and power—an image wrapped in oil and gold and diamonds and—

'I am American-Venezuelan by birth, but my roots are firmly planted in my Venezuelan links.'

And it hit. It hit with a sickening sense of understanding that made her sway where she stood.

'Ah,' he murmured. 'I see you are beginning to catch on. Yes, Miss Lacey,' he softly confirmed, 'Cristina

Alvarez is my sister. And you made the quick connection, I must assume, because your—affair with my brother-in-law took place in the DeSanquez apartment. The media made quite a meal out of these—juicy facts, did they not? In fact, their attention to detail was quite remarkably concise—the way they told of Annie Lacey lying with her lover in one bed while her lover's wife lay asleep in another bedroom of her brother's apartment. My apartment, Miss Lacey,' he enunciated thinly. 'My bed!'

Annie sank tremulously into a nearby chair, his anger, his contempt and his disgust breaking over her in cold, sickening waves while she fought with her own sense of anger and disgust—disgust for a single night in her life that would always, it seemed, come back to haunt her for as long as she lived.

She had gone to that apartment by invitation, to a party being held by a man called DeSanquez—a wealthy young Venezuelan who had expressed a desire to meet the sweet Angel Lacey, as everyone had called her then. She never had actually met the Venezuelan, she remembered now in surprise, because she hadn't given him a thought after meeting Alvarez instead.

Alvarez. She shuddered.

'Quite,' he observed. 'I acknowledge your horror. It was a revolting time for all of us. Not least my sister,' he pointed out. 'Having to walk into my bedroom and find you in my bed, not with me—it would not have mattered if it had been me,' he drawled. 'But to find you with her own husband was a terrible shock. It effectively ruined her marriage and ultimately almost ruined her life.

'For this alone,' he explained with a hateful coolness, 'I feel perfectly justified in demanding retribution from you—and indeed would have done so at the time this all happened if my sister had not begged me to let it be.

So, for Cristina's sake, and for Cristina's alone,' he made absolutely clear, 'I went against my personal desire to strangle the unscrupulous life out of you right there and then. But—that is not the end of it.'

Turning, he moved to place his coffee-cup on the top of the white marble fireplace then rested his arm alongside it. Every move he made, every unconscious gesture was so incredibly graceful that even in the middle of all of this Annie found herself drawn by him.

'I mentioned my dual nationality for a good reason,' he continued, his tone—as it had been throughout—utterly devoid of emotion. 'For although my father was Venezuelan my mother was, in actual fact, American. Now,' he asserted, as though relaying a mildly interesting piece of history, 'her name before she married my father was Frazer— Ah, I see you are quick. Yes.' He smiled thinly as Annie licked her suddenly dry lips. 'Susie is my cousin. Quite a coincidence, is it not, that you should happen to be the woman trying to ruin her life just as carelessly as you ruined my sister Cristina's?'

Annie closed her eyes, shutting out the crucifying blandness of his expression as he watched her. She had been wrong before when she'd believed him to be of the same ilk as Luis. He was in actual fact very different, if only because Luis had cared only for his own rotten neck while this man seemed to hold himself personally responsible for the necks of others.

Which in turn made him very dangerous because, in deciding to make himself an avenger, it was obvious that he was quite prepared to endanger his own neck to get retribution for those he loved. Blindly loved, she added heavily to herself. And she suddenly felt very, very sorry for him.

To each his Achilles heel, she mused starkly, opening her eyes to show him a perfectly cool expression. Luis Alvarez's Achilles heel had been his inflated ego, and the arrogant belief that power and money could buy for his bed any woman he'd desired. Cristina's had been her blindness to what her husband actually was. And Susie's was her need to have everything her selfish heart desired.

This man's was his fierce love for his family.

She then found herself wondering what her own Achilles heel was. She didn't know, but she had a horrible feeling that in this man's hands she was going to find out.

'You have nothing to say?' Her calmness was irritating him; she could see the annoyance begin to glint in his strange green eyes.

Green. 'No,' she answered. 'Not a single thing.' And another realisation hit her squarely in the face. Susie had green eyes—the same green eyes. Which seemed to tie the whole situation off neatly for her. She didn't have a cat-in-hell's chance of making this man with those eyes see anything from her point of view, so she wasn't even going to try. 'Perhaps you would, therefore, like to continue?' she invited, knowing with certainty that he had not offered her all of this information just for the fun of it.

His sudden burst of angry movement at her seeming indifference took her by surprise, because he had been so purposefully controlled up until then. His hand flicked down from the mantel, his body straightening tautly. 'Has nothing I have said managed to reach you?' he demanded harshly.

'It would seem not,' she said. 'All I've heard until now is a potted description of your family tree. Very interesting, I'm sure,' she drawled, 'but nothing for me to get fired up about.'

He didn't like it. He didn't like the fact that she could maintain a cool façade and even go as far as mocking him.

It served him right, she thought, for his arrogant supposition that he had a right to speak to her like this! If he had taken the trouble to find out about her—really find out instead of restricting his knowledge to pure tabloid gossip and the malicious judgement of his thankless family—then he would have discovered that few people managed to rile Annie Lacey with mere words. Out of sheer necessity she had grown a thick skin around herself to protect her from the cruel thrust of words, and it would take a better man than he to pierce that protective skin.

'When they say you possess none of the finer senses they are right, aren't they?' he muttered. 'Do you feel no hint of compassion for others at all?'

'It would seem not,' she said again, fielding his contempt with blue eyes that gave away nothing of what she was thinking or feeling inside. Then sheer devilment made her cock a golden eyebrow at him. 'Is there any in you?' she challenged right back.

'For you, you mean?' He shook his sleek dark head. 'No, Miss Lacey, I am sorry to inform you that I harbour not an ounce of compassion for you.'

'Then you have no right to expect more from me than you are willing to give yourself,' she said, and got up, her slender body no less sensuous in movement because it was stiff with control. He couldn't know, of course, that she had been through this kind of character-slaying before, and at far more lethal hands than his, or he would not be trying this tactic out on her.

'Where do you think you are going?' he demanded as she walked towards the door.

'Why, to the one place you obviously expect me to go,' she replied. 'To the devil. But by my route, Mr DeSanquez, I will do it by my own route.'

He moved like lightning, had to to reach the door even before she had a chance to turn the handle. His hand, big and slightly callused, closed around her own. Even with the light clasp he exerted, the hand managed to intimidate her.

'And how do you mean to get there?' he enquired silkily. 'Fly on your broomstick as witches do? Or are you more the snake, Miss Lacey, prepared to slither your way across the ocean to your devil's lair?'

'Funny,' she jeered, having to force herself to retaliate through the stifling breathlessness that she was suddenly experiencing at his closeness. 'But I thought this was the devil's lair?'

'I am merely his servant, Angelica,' he stated grimly. 'Merely his servant.'

There was nothing 'mere' about this man. He was larger than life itself—in size, in presence, in the sheer, physical threat of the man.

'I want to leave here,' she informed him coldly.

'But I've not finished with you yet.' The taunting words were murmured against her cheek, dampening her skin with his warm spicy breath.

'But I have finished with you!' she snapped, turning to anger to cover up the hectic effect his closeness was having on her. 'I demand that you fly me back to Union Island!' She tried to prise his fingers from her other hand. 'Now—before this silly game gets out of hand!'

He responded by snaking a hard arm around her waist and lifting her off the ground. Ignoring the way she twisted and struggled and kicked out with feet made ineffectual by the way he was carrying her, he walked over to the sofa and dropped her unceremoniously into the soft coral-coloured cushions, then came to lean threateningly over her.

'Now listen to me,' he commanded. 'And listen well, for this is no game. I mean business, Miss Lacey—serious business. You are here on my island for one purpose only, and that is to put you right out of circulation. From

now on I am going to ensure personally that you form
no danger to anyone in my family again!'

He was talking about Susie now, of course, Annie
realised. 'And how do you intend to do that?' she asked,
blue eyes flashing a scornful challenge at green, absolutely refusing to let him see how very frightened she was.
'By ruining my good reputation when everyone knows
I don't have one? Or do you have murder in mind, Mr
DeSanquez?' she taunted dangerously.

His anger flared at her refusal to take him seriously,
his bared teeth flashing bright white in a cruel dark face
as he reached for her again. 'Murder is too easy an escape
for you, you little she-devil,' he muttered. 'Perhaps this
will teach you to have a healthy fear of me!'

She didn't expect it, which was why he caught her so
totally off guard when his hard fingers curled tightly on
her shoulders and he brought her wrenchingly upwards
to meet the punishing force of his mouth.

It lasted only seconds, but it was long enough for her
to feel again the hectic sensation of her whole body
burning up, as though something totally alien had in-
vaded her.

She didn't move, did not so much as breathe or blink
an eyelash in response, yet, as she had been the evening
before, she was suddenly and excruciatingly aware of
him—aware of his strength, of the power behind the
muscles that strained angrily against her, of the subtle,
pleasing scent of him, the smooth texture of his tight,
tanned skin.

Her mouth was burning, her soft lips throbbing where
he pressed them bruisingly back against her tightly
clenched teeth. And her breasts—the damning traitors
that they were—were responding to the heated pressure
of his hard chest, the sensitive tips hardening into tight,
tingling sensors of pleasure as they pushed eagerly
towards him.

He muttered something in his throat and whipped a hand around the back of her neck so that he could arch her backwards, the other hand coming up between them to let a throbbing nipple push against his palm.

Annie gasped at the shocking insolence of the action, trying to pull away from him. But her gasp gave him entry into her mouth, and the next thing she knew she was being flung into a heady vortex of hot, moist intimacy.

Never—never since Alvarez—had she let a man kiss her like this. The very idea of it had always appalled her. But with this man it was the most achingly sensual experience of her life!

And that appalled her. It appalled her to know that she could be so receptive to a man who held her in such open contempt! And when he eventually lifted his head it was an act of sheer self-preservation that made her stare up at him with apparent indifference to the attack when in actual fact she was slowly and systematically collapsing inside.

'Well, well, well,' she heard herself murmur with an inner horror at her own gall. 'So you too are prepared to use sex to get what you want. And there I was, thinking you way above that kind of thing. How very disappointing.'

He stiffened violently at the taunt, then smiled ruefully when her meaning sank in. 'Ah,' he drawled. 'You are implying that we are similar creatures. But that is not the case,' he denied. 'You see, I do not sleep around—especially with promiscuous bitches who run a high risk of contamination.'

That cut—cut hard and deep. Not that she let him see it, her bruised and trembling mouth taking on a deriding twist as she taunted softly right back, 'Then I think you should tell your body that, because it seems to me that it's quite fancying a bit of contamination right now.' And she let her eyes drop to where the evidence of his own response to the kiss thrust powerfully against Annie's groin.

He dumped her so suddenly that she flailed back into the soft cushions behind her, but she barely noticed because her gaze was fixed incredulously on his hard, angry face.

He'd flushed—he'd actually flushed! She had absolutely thrown him by daring to point out his own sexual response, and elation at managing to get to him made her eyes flash with triumph.

Spinning away from her, he went to pour himself a drink—not coffee this time, but something stronger from a crystal decanter standing on a beautiful mahogany sideboard by the fireplace.

Annie got to her feet, studying him with more curiosity than fear now as that small revelation helped her to diminish the godlike proportions she had been allowing herself to see in him.

How old was he? she found herself wondering curiously. Thirty-one—thirty-two? Not much older, she was certain, though her original impression last night—had it only been last night?—had been of a much older, more mature man.

'Don't you think it's time you told me exactly what it is you do want from me?' she suggested when the silence began to drag between them.

He turned with glass in hand. 'What I want from you is quite simple,' he said, having got his temper back under control, she noted. 'I want you taken right out of Hanson's life, and I intend personally to make sure it happens.'

Todd? She stared at him, amazed that she could have forgotten all about Todd! Even when he'd brought Susie into this Annie had only connected the other girl with their modelling war. Susie's connection with Todd had not even entered her head!

Stupid! she berated herself. How damned stupid can you get? Of course this was all about Todd and Susie, and not just Susie and the *Cliché* contract!

It was like being on a see-saw, she likened heavily. One minute feeling the uplift of her own confidence returning before she crashed down again so abruptly that she was starting to feel dizzy.

'How long have you known Hanson?' he asked her suddenly.

Almost all my life, Annie thought, with a smile that seemed to soften the whole structure of her face. Then she shrugged, slender shoulders shifting inside the white cotton top. 'None of your business,' she said.

He grimaced, as if acknowledging her right to be uncooperative. Yet he tried again—on a slightly different tack. 'But you have been lovers on an off for—what—four years, is it now?'

'No comment.'

He took a sip at his drink, green eyes thoughtful as they ran slowly over her. Annie fixed him with a bland stare; she was determined to give him no help whatsoever.

'You are very beautiful,' he remarked, making her eyelashes flicker in memory of the way he had said that to her the night before. 'Incredibly so for someone who has led such a chequered life. It is no wonder my brother-in-law lost his head over you.'

'Something you are determined not to do,' she reminded him, smiling although the fact that just thinking of Luis Alvarez was enough to turn her stomach.

'And Hanson,' he continued, as if she had not spoken. 'He cannot seem to help himself where you are concerned.'

'Is this conversation supposed to be leading somewhere?' she asked. 'Only, if it is, would you kindly get to the point so I can get out of here? I am tired and would like to get off this island so I can book into a hotel somewhere and get some sleep tonight.'

'Oh, you will get your sleep, Miss Lacey,' he assured her smoothly. 'Plenty of it—in the bed already waiting for you upstairs. You see...' He paused—entirely for effect, Annie suspected. 'As from tonight you became my mistress, and therefore will sleep wherever I sleep.'

'*What*—?' Annie began to laugh. She couldn't help it; the whole thing was getting so ridiculous that she was truly beginning to believe that she must be stuck in some real-as-life nightmare—one of those where nothing made any sense!

'Oh, not in the physical sense of the word,' he inserted coolly into her laughter, 'since we have already established that I have no wish to go where too many men have been before me.'

'Have we?' Her blue eyes mocked him. He lifted his chin and ignored the silent taunt.

'It is, therefore, simple logic to assume that I mean to create the illusion of intimacy—solely for the minds of others.'

'And I'm supposed to meekly go along with all of this, am I?' she murmured with rueful scorn.

Funnily enough, instead of getting angry with her again, he grimaced. 'No,' he conceded. 'Not meekly, I do acknowledge. But I fail to see what you can do about it since this is my island, and the only form of transport off it is in my helicopter. And,' he continued while Annie grimly took all of that in, 'considering I hold the very success of Hanson's launch into Europe in the palm of my hand, I think I can—persuade you to do exactly what I want you to do. If only for Hanson's sake,' he added carefully.

Annie's spine straightened slowly, her attention well and truly fixed now. 'What is that supposed to mean?' she demanded.

'Exactly what it said.' He rid himself of his glass then shoved his hands into the pockets of his lightweight trousers. The action drew her eyes unwillingly downwards to that place where the evidence of his arousal had been so obviously on show.

Not so now. The man was back in control of his body, his stance supremely relaxed. 'As I suppose you must already know, Hanson has overstretched his resources going into Europe,' he went on smoothly. 'He is in dire need of a world exclusive to get his new magazine off the ground. Convincing me to let him publish my new collection is undoubtedly that world exclusive. Using your body to display that collection means he cannot fail. And indeed,' he went on while Annie stood taking it all in, 'I have no wish for him to fail. It would not suit my cousin, you see, for the man she loves to be a failure,' he pointed out. 'But,' he then warned chillingly, 'I am prepared to have him fail if you are not prepared to do exactly what I say.'

The bottom line, Annie recognised as he fell into a meaningful silence. They had just reached the bottom line—as far as any protest from her went anyway. Because from the moment he said he was able to hurt Todd she had been beaten. She would do anything for Todd. Lay down her life for Todd.

Prostitute herself for Todd.

'Tell me exactly what you want me to do,' she said huskily, and at last gave him his victory over her spirit by letting her shoulders wilt in defeat.

Oddly, rather than pleasing him it seemed to have the opposite effect, tightening his mouth and putting an impatient glint into his strange green eyes.

'Look,' he exhaled irritably, 'why don't you avail yourself of some of that coffee? You are obviously jet lagged and no doubt dehydrated. Please...' He waved a hand towards the trolley, but when she still just stood there, looking like a slowly wilting flower, another sigh rasped from him and he came to grasp her arm, guiding her to one of the chairs and pushing her roughly into it.

Annie glanced at the hand on her arm, long-fingered and beautifully sculptured, then at his face, darkly intense and intimidatingly grim, and shivered, realising just how accurate her first impression of this man had been. Danger, her instincts had warned her. Danger—hard with resolve.

Dangerous on several levels, she acknowledged as her senses quivered beneath his touch. Then, as she let her tense body relax into the chair, she was filled with a sudden aching kind of sadness. For the first time in her adult life she had come upon a man whom she did not feel an instant physical revulsion for, and he wanted only to do her harm.

Lifting her hand, she began rubbing at her brow with weary fingers. Her head was beginning to ache, the long hours of travelling only to be faced with all of... this beginning to take their toll.

A minute later a cup of strong coffee was placed into her hand, then he stood over her, with those piercing eyes probing her pale face while she sipped at the strong, sweet drink.

'Please explain the rest,' she requested, once the drink had managed to warm a small part of her numbed body.

He looked ready to refuse, an oddly ferocious look tightening his lean face. Then, on a short sigh, he turned away. 'Hanson will get his exclusive for his magazine,' he assured her. 'Only—' he turned back to face her '—it won't be you wearing the Adamas collection, it will be Susie—after Hanson has begged me to allow her to take your place, of course, when you don't turn up in time for his deadline because you have disappeared with your lover.'

'You, I suppose.' Her smile was twisted with contempt.

'Of course.' He gave an arrogant half-nod of his dark head. 'It has to be convincing, after all. The man may have overstretched his resources in this economic climate, but he is no fool. He knows you well enough to suspect anything less than your assurance that the love of a very rich man has brought this decision on you.'

He paused, waiting for her to put up a protest or at least show some horrified response to his demands. But when she revealed nothing—nothing whatsoever—his frown came back, the first hint of puzzlement showing on his rock-solid, certain face.

'You understand what I am demanding of you?' he questioned. 'I am demanding that you cut yourself completely free of Hanson—both professionally and personally. No contact,' he made clear. 'Nothing. He loves my cousin, but he suffers an incurable lust for you. You cannot be allowed to go on ruining lives simply because that body of yours drives men insane!'

And whose fault is that? she wondered cynically. Mine for projecting exactly what they want to see? Or theirs for being such pathetic slaves to their wretched libidos?

She glanced at him from beneath her lashes, wondering curiously if this man had ever been a slave to his libido. And decided not. He was Adamas—the rock, the invincible one! And just too damned proud to let himself become a slave to anything—except his family, maybe.

And there, she realised suddenly, was his weakness! Hers was Todd and always would be Todd. His was his pride and abiding love for his family.

'You know...' she murmured thoughtfully, a small seed of an idea beginning to develop in her mind. If it worked—if she could swing it—there was a small chance that she could get herself out of this relatively un-scathed. 'You've forgotten one rather obvious thing in all your careful planning,' she said. 'If, by your reck-oning, I've had Todd at my beck and call for the last four years, despite the countless other men he knows have been falling in and out of my bed—then he isn't going to give up on me just because you've come along.'

That deep sense of personal pride took the shape of haughty arrogance on his face. 'He will if I insist upon it,' he said.

'Enough to make him turn to Susie for comfort?' she charged. 'Enough to make him thrust me from his mind? I'm sorry—' ruefully she shook her head '—but it won't happen. Todd loves me, you see,' she stated with a soft and sincere certainty. 'Loves me from the heart not the body. Or why else do you think he keeps coming back to me no matter what goes on in my life?

'Ask Susie if you don't believe me,' she prompted when deriding scepticism that anyone could love a pro-miscuous bitch like her turned his attractive mouth ugly. 'Ask her why all her other attempts to make Todd dismiss me from his life have failed. And ask yourself why a beautiful, desirable woman like Susie cannot win her man on her terms without having to bring you in to do it for her.

'Ask her—' she gently thrust her strongest point home '—if she's ever asked Todd why he refuses to give me up, and if she's honest, Mr DeSanquez, she'll tell you that she *has* asked him, and Todd had told her, quite clearly, that he loves me and will always love me until the day he dies—no matter what I do.'

Silence. She had him wondering, and Annie had to stifle the urge to smile in triumph. The way his sleek black brows were pulling downwards over the bridge of his long, thin nose told her that she had forced him to consider what she'd said.

'You could keep me here for six months—a year! but when I eventually went back Todd would be waiting for me with open arms. Is Susie prepared to live with that?' she challenged. 'Knowing that, no matter how deeply she manages to inveigle Todd into her clutches, I will always be there like the shadowed wings of a hawk in their lives, waiting to swoop down and steal him right away from her?'

This felt good—really good! Annie thought with relish as he spun restlessly away. He poured another drink, swallowed it down in one go then turned, forcing her to smooth the pleased glow out of her eyes as he glanced sharply back at her.

'You really are the shrewd, calculating bitch my family label you, are you not?' he said grimly.

'I am what I am.' She shrugged, throwing his own words of earlier right back at him.

'And what made you what you are, I wonder?' he mused angrily.

'Oh, that's easy,' she said. 'There's a final ingredient in all of this which should clear that up.' She looked him straight in the eye. 'You see, I love Todd in exactly the same way that he loves me. Only, we are not allowed to show it because of Todd's mother. You do know who Todd's mother is, don't you?' she questioned tauntingly.

'She is Lady Sarah Hanson,' she provided the answer whether he knew it or not. 'A woman with pure blue aristocratic blood running through her veins. She would die rather than see her son align himself with a woman with my reputation.' Her soft mouth twisted on that little truism.

'Lady Sarah also suffers from a chronic heart condition,' she went on. Most of this was the absolute truth—most of it. 'Todd is strong—tough—but draws the line at killing his own mother.' She gave a helpless shrug. 'Your Susie doesn't stand a chance against a love like ours, Mr DeSanquez,' she concluded, 'and you would be doing her a bigger service by telling her that, rather than trying to blackmail me.'

At that she got up, mentally crossing her fingers that she'd managed to swing it. He was certainly not as confident as he had been, nor—oddly—as contemptuous of her as he studied her thoughtfully.

'No.' He shook his dark head and her heart sank. 'You are wrong. I have seen the way he looks at my cousin, and no matter what you believe about his feelings for you Hanson gazes at her like a man angrily frustrated in love. Whatever hold you may have on him, and I do not deny it is there,' he conceded, 'I think it is time— perhaps more than time—that both you and Hanson learned to forget each other.

'I saw the way you were with him the other night, watched the seductive way you utterly bewitched him, seducing him with your promising smiles and the sensual brush of your exquisite body.' Contemptuously his gaze raked over her. 'Susie has a chance with him with you out of the way,' he concluded. 'She stands none while you are around.'

'So what is your plan?' she scoffed at him deridingly, her mind tumbling over itself in an effort to find the hidden key that would stop all of this. 'To keep me here tonight and tomorrow night and the next and the next in the hopes that it will blacken me in his eyes? Didn't you hear a word I said?' she sighed. 'Todd doesn't care what I do or who I do it with! He will forgive me for you and he will forgive me for breaking my contract with *Cliché*!'

'Then you have a rather big problem on your hands, Miss Lacey,' he countered grimly. 'Because if you do not find a way of convincing him that you care nothing for him any more then I withdraw my support for his magazine. So now what do you suggest that we do?'

Catch twenty-two. Annie felt her heart sink in her breast.

# CHAPTER FIVE

'I SEE I have managed to silence that quick little tongue of yours,' he taunted when the silence stretched out between them. 'But I would appreciate a suggestion as to how we overcome the stalemate we seem to have created.'

'I don't have one,' Annie admitted dully, eyes lowered so that he wouldn't see the frustration glittering there.

'I see,' he said silkily. 'Then it seems to be up to me to find it for you. That is, of course,' he then prompted, 'if you are prepared to do anything to save Hanson from ruin?'

'Yes,' she whispered, with a numbness that encompassed her whole being.

'I beg your pardon?' he drawled aggravatingly, coming to lean over her, bracing his hands on the arms of her chair. 'Was that a yes? I did not quite catch the word.'

'Yes—it was a yes!' she flared, her fingers clenching into tight fists of frustration on her lap. 'I'll do anything to save Todd from ruin!' Then, on a sudden flood of tears that blurred her beautiful eyes, she choked, 'Anything, damn you—anything!'

It was odd, but the tears seemed to throw him. His eyes widened, shocked surprise showing on his lean face before he suddenly jerked away from her as if those tears held poison in them and he was afraid of dying if they so much as touched his skin.

But anyone who knew Annie well would also have known that when tears flowed from her eyes so did her temper burn up to counteract them, and she jumped from her seat, those same tears glistening with a wretched, bitter anger.

'So what do you want me to do?' she demanded shrilly. 'Strip naked in public in the hopes I'll make him despise me? Or simply cut my own throat and put a quick end to all poor Susie's problems? Or maybe,' she went on while he just seemed to stand there struck by her sudden explosion, 'you would like me to strip naked in public *and* cut my own throat? That should do it!' she concluded thickly. 'Put a neat if messy end to the whole bloody lot!'

'Swearing doesn't help,' he said, as if that one expletive was the only part of what she'd thrown at him that had actually meant anything at all.

'Hah!' she choked, her temper almost shooting right out of the top of her head, then disappearing suddenly when she began to see the black humour of the situation. Here she was, offering to top herself for that cat Susie's sake! She couldn't believe that she could be sunk so low!

'I do not think we need take such drastic action—on either point,' he added calmly.

Or was it calmingly? Annie focused her eyes on him at last, wary of the expression on his face that was neither gleeful nor, as she would have expected, contemptuous, but strangely—

No. She spun her back on him, arms wrapping tightly around her body in an age-old gesture of self-defence. She refused so much as to put a word to what her senses had told her that new look in his eyes meant!

'Then what the hell *do* you want me to do?' she muttered thickly.

There was a silence behind her that made the fine nerves lying along her spine prickle. She closed her eyes tightly, refusing—refusing to listen to what her senses were screaming at her. It was impossible. No man could find it arousing to have a woman swap insults with him! No woman could find it arousing to spar with a man like him!

Yet—

Oh, God, if he touched her now... And she could feel him fighting the urge to do just that, feel it with every instinct she possessed buzzing in warning that he was—

'You must convince Hanson that I mean more to you than he does.' The words came from a throat roughened by the battle he had just fought with himself and won. 'You must make him believe that I am the man who has managed to take his place in your heart!'

Annie had to swallow to clear the tension from her throat. 'And how am I supposed to do that?' she asked, without turning to face him. She didn't dare.

Didn't dare.

Another loaded pause shifted the tension upwards another notch. Then he said quietly, 'In two weeks Hanson will arrive here at my invitation. You will first convince him that you and I have become—passionate lovers, then I will hand him an envelope which will supposedly contain the photographs he desires so much. But before he has a chance to open it you will take it from him and rip it in two.'

'*What*?' That made her turn, her blue eyes dark with confusion as she levelled them at him. 'But what is that going to prove?' she gasped.

'It will prove that your love for me means more to you than your love for him, because you are prepared to ruin him rather than lose me. You see,' he went on, turning slightly to pick up his glass, 'I will have issued you with a decision to make. You can save him and lose me, or ruin him and have me. You will, of course, choose me.'

'But—I thought the whole point of all of this was *not* to ruin Todd?' she choked, utterly bewildered now.

'No—no,' he denied. 'The whole point of all of this is to pay you back for the ruin you have wrought in others' lives and to get you out of Hanson's life,' he corrected. 'And your taking away his best chance at success at the eleventh hour should alienate you completely,' he decreed with grim satisfaction.

'But will also lose you my agreement to co-operate,' she said. 'Or have you forgotten that I'm only doing this for Todd's sake?'

'No.' He shook his dark head. 'I have not forgotten. But you seem to have forgotten my cousin Susie waiting in the wings to step neatly into your shoes. Co-operate, and she will convince me to let her take your place. Susie will wear the Adamas collection for *Cliché*'s European launch, save Hanson from ruin and receive his undying gratitude in the interim. Refuse to co-operate,' he added smoothly, 'and I will simply keep you here out of harm's way until the very last moment—then pull out of the deal—' he gave an idle shrug '—leaving him with nothing—nothing to fall back on. You understand?'

Understand? Oh, yes, she understood, Annie thought bitterly. Susie gets everything at Annie Lacey's expense.

'My God!' she breathed. 'You're worse than Svengali, aren't you? And what happens to me once this little charade is all over?' she asked. 'Am I supposed to keep my mouth shut about the way you and Susie plotted this whole thing against me? Because I won't, Mr DeSanquez,' she warned him angrily. 'And by then *Cliché* will be launched and you won't be able to hurt Todd!'

His answering sigh was harsh and driven. 'Why can you not possess enough simple decency to see without the threats that it is time you let go of Hanson—for his sake if not your own?'

'You talk to me about decency,' she countered scathingly. 'Where is yours while you stand here threatening me like this?'

'You need teaching a lesson,' he muttered, but she knew that her words had got through to him because he dropped his gaze from hers.

'Not in Susie Frazer's name, I don't,' she denied. 'And you're wrong to do this to me and wrong to do this to Todd simply on the evidence of that silly, deranged woman!'

Wrong thing to say, Annie realised as anger flared into his vivid green eyes and he took a threatening step towards her. 'You will take that back!' he insisted, thrusting his dark face close to her own.

For once he looked and sounded completely foreign—hard and dark and frighteningly alien, his anger so palpable that she could almost taste it. Annie quailed inside but refused to show it, her blue eyes clinging defiantly to his.

'I will take nothing back!' she spat at him. 'In your arrogant self-righteousness you like to believe that I've sinned against your rotten family when in reality it is they who've sinned against me!'

'Sin?' he repeated. 'You are sin, Annie Lacey. With your siren's body and your lush, lying mouth.'

'The lies are all yours, Adamas,' she threw back. 'And what do you think it will do to Susie's chances when Todd finds out what a lie this whole thing actually is?'

'And you intend to tell him so?' he demanded.

Annie stood firm in her defiance. 'What do you expect me to do once this is all over?' she snapped. 'Crawl into some dark corner and pretend I no longer exist? I have a life waiting for me out there, Mr DeSanquez. You can put it on hold for a few short weeks but not for ever! And, my God, I vow that the first thing I'll do with that life is save Todd from Susie's calculating clutches if it becomes the very last thing I am able to do!'

His anger shot up another notch, sent there, she suspected, by sheer frustration with her for defying him like this. 'By telling Hanson the truth?' He was demanding confirmation.

'About your lies? Yes!' she declared.

His hand whipped out, curling threateningly around the back of her neck. 'Then we will have to make the lies the truth,' he gritted, moving close so that his body pressed along the full length of hers. His breath was warm against her face, his green eyes glowing with a new and terrifyingly readable light. 'I shall bed you if I have to, Angelica Lacey,' he told her huskily. 'I will take your beautiful body and drown in its sinful lusts every night for the next two weeks if you continue to insist on telling the truth.'

'No,' she protested, trying to move away from him. The heat from his body was having a strange effect on her own, burning it, bringing it to life, disturbing all those delicate senses she had always so thoroughly locked away.

'Why not?' he whispered. 'Why not make the charade the truth? Two weeks is a long time for a woman like you to go without a man. And I find I am man enough to be—receptive to your charms. Why not?' he repeated, almost as though he was trying to convince himself rather than her. His mouth lowered to brush a tantalising caress along her cheek. 'I can feel you trembling,' he murmured. 'I can feel your breasts throbbing against my chest, smell the sweet scent of desire on your skin. You want me, Angelica.'

'No—'

'Yes,' he insisted. 'As much as I admit to wanting you.'

'No—' she denied again, trying to pull free because he was conjuring up all kinds of sensations that were totally, frighteningly foreign to her.

'You want proof?' Reaching down, he took hold of her tightly clenched hands and grimly prised the fingers apart before forcing by sheer superior strength her tense palm to press against the hardening muscle between his thighs. 'Proof,' he muttered, and captured her shaken gasp with his hungry mouth.

For a few blinding, ecstatic moments Annie let herself sink willingly into the embrace, some small, sensible corner of her brain telling her that this had been coming from the moment they'd met the night before, that the violent exchange of words had merely been a vent for... this—this sudden greedy need to feel his mouth on hers again, to feel his body pulse against her, know his touch, his taste, the texture of his tight, tanned skin.

But it was only for a few hectic moments, then an icy darkness began closing her in—the darkness of bad memories, of man's physical power over woman and his ability to subdue her if she dared to protest.

And suddenly, instead of the warm, coaxing mouth of the man kissing her now, she was being stifled by the hot, wet pressure of another mouth—a cruel mouth—and cruel hands that hurt as they touched her. Hands which had her crying out, fighting for breath, straining to get free, struggling—struggling so desperately that she didn't even know that she was flailing wildly at César DeSanquez with her fists, didn't realise that he was no longer kissing her but frowning down at her, no longer holding her in an embrace but trying—unsuccessfully— to stop her from landing blows on his surprised face.

'Angel—'

It was all she heard. Not the full 'Angelica' he had actually said in husky concern but 'Angel' as Luis had husked at her—'Angel. I have a real angel in my bed.'

'No!' she ground out, and managed at last to break free, her blue eyes wild as she turned like a terrified animal and ran.

Ran out of the open windows across the veranda and down the wooden steps. Ran—ran with no idea where she was running as her feet took her across the springy grass still warm from the long day's sun. It was almost dark outside now, but she didn't notice—didn't notice anything as she made her mindless bid for escape.

She came to a halt only when the balmy water of the Caribbean lapped around her thighs. Breathless from running, panting with fear, she lifted her dazed eyes to the miles of coral-washed water laid out in front of her and at last felt reality return.

Not Luis Alvarez but César DeSanquez. Not the darkened bedroom of a plush London penthouse but a Caribbean island basking in the embrace of a beautiful dying sun.

'Oh, God,' she choked out thickly. 'Oh, God.' And, limp-limbed suddenly, she dropped like a weighted sack onto her knees, then as the water closed in a lazy, silken swirl around her heaving shoulders she put her hands to her face and wept.

Whatever he would do about her stupid flight she didn't consider, but certainly she didn't expect him to come wading into the water after her, his dark eyes tight with fury as he hauled her angrily to her feet and began dragging her back onto dry land again.

It was only later that it occurred to her that it might well have looked to him as if she were trying to drown herself. Whatever, it gained her no sympathy whatsoever—no hint of remorse as he muttered something harsh and Spanish beneath his breath then picked her up in his arms and carried her back up the garden towards the house.

His step hardly altered as he carried her up a flight of steps that led up the outside wall of the house and along the upper balcony into a room where he dropped her onto her unsteady feet before stalking off towards what she vaguely assumed was a bathroom.

Because this was a bedroom, she realised on yet another rise of panic—a bedroom with two full-length windows standing open either side of a huge coral-pink covered bed.

'Get those wet things off!' He came back with a fluffy white towel. Annie started, her blue eyes huge in her pale face as she stared blankly at him, unable to move a single muscle in case she fell down again.

With another Spanish curse he began stripping off her clothes, the bite of his fingers quelling any attempt she made at trying to stop him. She was shivering violently, though with shock rather than cold. Her top came off and was thrown down on the soft coral-coloured carpet, her arms wrenched away when they automatically crossed over her breasts. With rough hands he unclipped her bra and sent that flying too.

Then, as she stood there still half-numbed by her mind-blowing reaction to his kiss, the towel landed around her shoulders and he was kneeling in front of her, dark face stern as he ruthlessly began to strip the dripping wet skirt from her, followed instantly by her briefs.

'You stupid fool,' he bit out hoarsely. 'What made you do something as crazy as that?'

She didn't answer—couldn't. She just stood there huddling into the towel and shivering so badly that her teeth chattered. He cursed again, turning angrily away, and began wrenching off his own sodden clothes. His trousers landed on top of her skirt, the sleek, lean flanks of his buttocks flexing as he stripped away his briefs and sent them the same way before spinning back to face her, arrogant in his complete lack of modesty and misreading her new, white-faced stillness as indifference to his exposure while he railed at her once again.

'I should throttle the lovely life out of you for doing something as stupid as that!'

With another rasping sigh he turned and walked back into the bathroom while Annie stood staring after him, mesmerised by those exposed buttocks rippling as he moved. He came back with another towel, his face no less angry as he stripped his shirt over his head and slammed it down onto the floor.

And Annie lost the ability to breathe.

Her eyes were fixed unblinkingly on that daunting juncture between muscle-taut thighs where the shadowing of crisp black chest hair arrowed to a thick cluster around his potent sex.

He obviously felt no qualms about standing stark naked in front of Annie Lacey. As far as he was concerned, she had seen it all before—many times. But to her this was one of the most critical occasions of her life. And she could neither move, breathe nor speak as, dry-mouthed, she stared at him, horrified by the slow, rumbling burn beginning to erupt deep down inside her.

Desire—for a man who held her in such contempt. And a fascination so strong that she couldn't even make herself look the other way! Her eyes flickered, then shifted to graze over wide shoulders and bulging biceps where the deeply tanned skin shone like lovingly oiled leather.

His chest was wide and firm, covered by the thick mass of black curling hair—hair that angled down over a stomach so tight that she felt she could throw a punch at it and not make it give so much as a fraction. Then those hips—those narrow, tight hips so arrogantly cradling the essence of the man himself, a man endowed with such power that she could almost feel its—

'*Santa María . . .*'

The softly uttered words barely impinged on her concentration. She was too lost in what was happening to him, too busy watching in paralysed awe as his body stirred, hardened, grew into full masculine arousal.

He let go of the towel and began walking slowly towards her. Annie took in a short, shaky breath and moistened her dry lips with her tongue. She couldn't move, was unable to do anything other than watch him fill with desire, and feel her own senses fill with the same.

'Sin,' he muttered tightly as his eyes glittered over her. 'You are sin, Angelica Lacey. Pure sin.'

Coming to a stop in front of her, his hand lifted, stroking across her shoulder on its way to capture the edge of her towel. She was trembling when it fell away—not shivering now, but most definitely trembling. There was a subtle difference, and it all had to do with the sensations she was experiencing inside.

His hand was on her waist, gripping, tugging—arrogant in his maleness as he lifted her up against him. She arched on an indrawn gasp as his manhood slid proudly between her trembling thighs. For a moment they stayed like that, their eyes locked, burning, darkened by feeling. Then he captured her parted mouth, widened it and plunged hungrily in.

And she surrendered—surrendered to the storm that had been building steadily from the moment their eyes had clashed across a crowded room...

Nothing—nothing in her vast and cynical if second-hand knowledge about the act of love had prepared her for what had actually taken place there in the growing darkness of that night.

Nothing. And she lay very still beside the man who had just propelled her into true womanhood, not daring to move while she came to terms with the wreck it had left of her emotions—her senses! Her very soul.

César was lying beside her, stretched out on his stomach, his arms curved tensely around his dark head. His body was damp, layered with a fine film of perspiration. His shoulders, his hips, his slim, tight buttocks were trembling as he struggled to come to terms with what had just taken place.

He was shocked.

Dear God, *she* was shocked! But both for different reasons. She was shocked by the sheer, brutal reality of the act. His shock came from discovering that the woman he had just taken with such devastating power and sensuality was not the woman he had believed her to be.

And why should he have suspected? she asked herself bitterly. She was the notorious Annie Lacey, for goodness' sake. Used—more than used to experiencing what they had just done!

She had not even attempted to tell him the truth.

And would he have believed the truth if she had attempted to tell him?

Of course not. Who would? She was Annie Lacey. A product of her own making. She had set out to build a lie around herself and had succeeded so successfully that no one ever thought of questioning that lie.

But he could have been—kinder, she thought on a sudden well of anguish. No matter who or what he'd believed her to be, he still could have been kinder— couldn't he?

Tears lay like a film across her eyes, blurring her vision as the moon filtered through the darkness of the room. She hurt. She hurt in so many places that she did not know which one hurt the most—her body, still wearing the power of his physical imprint, her brain, grinding against her skull in stunned revelation, her senses, still quivering, flailing around in the morass of the aftermath, not quite knowing what had happened to them, and too shattered by it all even to attempt to regroup.

Then a hand reached out to touch her, and everything—mind, body, shattered senses—leapt upwards and together in a wild dovetailing of panic, sending her rolling from the bed to land, swaying, on her feet—feet that were already stumbling away, running from what she knew was bound to come next.

The post-mortem. No! Please! Just let me be!

Bathroom. A bathroom door had a lock on it, and she needed to put herself behind lock and key before he—

'Angelica...'

No! Bright balls of panic propelled themselves against the back of her eyes, and in one swift movement she leapt like a gazelle into the bathroom, closing and locking the door behind her before sliding heavily down its smooth, panelled white surface onto the cold, hard ceramic-tiled floor.

Her knees came up, her arms wrapping tensely around them, then her head was lowering, the silken tangle of her hair falling like a curtain all around her as she sat huddled, shivering. Exposed.

Exposed for exactly what she was.

A fraud.

For the last four years of her life she had been a complete fraud. She, the shrewd and cynical Annie Lacey, who had believed that she was playing a great game with other people's perception of her, now realised that she had only been deceiving herself. In her way, she'd believed that she was punishing them all for making her be that way when in actual fact she had been punishing herself—punishing herself for a whole range of things, Alvarez being only a small part in all of that, she now realised.

He had been the conductor, but not the whole orchestra.

'Oh, God.' The words came choking from a throat closed tight on tears of self-knowledge.

You hate yourself, Annie, she told herself wretchedly—not all those other people who only responded to what you gave them to respond to. You built Annie Lacey because you truly believe that persona the only one you're fit for.

Woman as whore. She shuddered nauseously. The fact that you never actually did whore around is incidental. It is what you believed yourself to be.

And now you are, she added starkly—the whore of a man who despises everything about you, even the fact that he could not stop himself from devouring the body he despised so much.

'Sin'. He had called her 'sin'.

'Angelica.' A tap at the door behind her accompanied the gruff reverberation of her name. 'Angelica, open the door.'

No. God, no, she thought, and stumbled to her feet, blue eyes so dark with emotion that they seemed black in her paste-white face. Sheer instinct sent her towards the glass door which housed the shower cubicle. She stepped in and switched on the jet, not caring that the water hissed down icy cold on top of her, then almost immediately stinging-hot.

The need to wash away the whole experience kept her locked beneath the shower, lost to everything but a grinding knowledge of utter self-disgust.

If he knocked or called her name again, she didn't hear him. And she stayed like that for long, long minutes, face lowered, water streaming onto her head until her long hair split and hung in two slick golden pelts from her nape.

Then, slowly, a sense of feeling began to creep back into her numbed flesh, the hot sting of water pulsing down on her urging her back to life, and she lifted her head, found a bar of soap and began methodically washing herself. Toes, feet, legs. Her thighs where his thrusting body had left marks on her fine, delicate skin.

She washed her hips and her buttocks—sore where the height of his passion had sent his fingers digging in. The smell of him and the feel of him still lingered languorously in the hot, steamy air.

Her belly felt tight and tender inside, her breasts alien parts of her that, when she smoothed soap over the taut, swollen mounds, brought a sharp gasp of reaction from her tight throat as her fingers brushed nipples still erect and raw from his hot, hungry kisses.

He had left his mark here in other ways too—in reddened blotches where his lips had nipped and sucked. Her throat had the same—several tender places where she knew she would bruise later on. It was the way of her skin—pale, delicate, it bruised at the slightest knock.

Her arms seemed to be the only part of her that had escaped the marks of his possession—except for her wrists, she noted as she stared at them, ringed pink where he had gripped them together over her head. Oh, not in a demand for submission, she grimly allowed, but in rough, angry passion. He'd wanted to stretch her out to her fullest so that he could taste every inch of her skin with his tongue, kneeling over her with his dark face fierce with desire.

A ripple fluttered over her skin—in memory of the pleasure he had given. Her mouth, full and throbbing, was still wearing his kisses even though she had washed her lips as well.

Sighing, she turned her face up to the spray then stood there with her eyes closed, trying not to think of it any more.

Then her nails curled tensely into her palms as unwillingly she remembered what she had done to him, how the wild explosion of passion inside her had sent her fingers raking across his sleekly groomed head, searching for, finding and clutching at the slim tail of hair, then tugging—using it to pull him closer so that she could lose herself in his hot, marauding mouth.

Then later... She shuddered, remembering how those same fingers had scraped the ribbon right away, his hair falling like midnight silk around her as her fingers had moved on again, curling into tense claws to score down the full length of his long, muscular back as he'd entered her... Her impassioned cry of pain echoed now in the hollow place her mind had become.

Well, there was one thing, she mocked herself grimly when eventually she made herself move again, she had gone from virgin to experienced lover in one fell swoop, because there had been nothing that he hadn't shown her in that wildly hectic romp on the bed, nothing he had not been prepared to do to heighten their pleasure.

No gentle introduction for the virgin. No holds barred.

That point between her thighs quivered in response, and jerkily she pushed herself out of the shower before it all took too frightening a grip on her again.

Another huge white bath sheet hung folded on the rail. Picking it up, she wrapped it fully around herself then found another towel which she wrapped turban-style round her head.

It took a teeth-clenching gathering together of all her courage to make her unlock the door and step back into the bedroom.

# CHAPTER SIX

CÉSAR WAS still there, standing by the open window on the other side of the bed, gazing out at a moonlit sea. He was dressed again, in a fresh white shirt and a pair of casual trousers. His hair had been severely contained once again.

Like the man, she decided hollowly—back under control.

Someone had removed the wet clothes, and the bed had been tidied. Not that it mattered. Nothing mattered.

Ignoring him, she moved over to a big, apricot-coloured easy chair and, snatching up the scatter cushion lying on it, sat down, curling herself into it, hugging the cushion to her breasts.

'Why?' he demanded quietly—nothing else. It really was not necessary to add anything else.

'People see what they want to see,' she answered flatly. She could have said more but didn't. She didn't want to talk at all. She just wanted to sit here and wallow in the aftermath of a holocaust.

He moved, turning his tense body a little so that he could look at her. The movement made her glance warily at him, her huge blue eyes that had lost all their self-protecting veils clashing with a tight, grim face emptied of most of its beautiful colour. He was holding his lips in a straight, tight line, as if the teeth behind them were fiercely clenched, his chiselled jaw set under the pressure.

His eyes were dark and sombre, the truth overlaying his earlier contempt with remorse.

No. She looked down and away again as compassion for him began to swell inside her. But she was too full with her own dark thoughts just now to deal with his.

And anyway, even though she was aware that maybe half of the blame for what had taken place between them had to lie at her own feet—or those of the Annie Lacey she had so carefully deceived everyone with—she could not forgive him his soulless seduction.

Would not forgive him.

He had got her here to this island under false pretences. He had insulted and threatened her, then coolly blackmailed her before offering the final indignity of ruthlessly seducing her.

If he'd wanted his revenge, he had it. She only hoped that he was satisfied with his results.

Oh, God help me, she thought on a sudden well of absolute despair, and began to sob softly, brokenly into the protection of the cushion.

'Hell.' The thickened curse came from very close by. He was squatting down in front of her. 'I'm sorry,' he murmured deeply. 'What else can I say? I swear to you, I never meant to hurt you like this.'

No? He had set out to hurt her from the very moment they'd met. If it hadn't been this way then it would have been another. He'd seen only the persona, which made the rest of what had happened such a sick joke because, in the end, even he hadn't been able to keep his hands off Annie Lacey, the super-tramp.

And the angry way he'd lost control of himself had told her just how much he'd despised himself for it.

'Leave me alone,' she whispered. 'I just w-want to be left alone.'

He sighed, the heavy sound disturbing the air around her naked shoulders and she shivered.

'You're cold,' he said, with a kind of rough gentleness that made her want to weep all the more. 'Let me help you into bed, then I will—'

'No!' His hand had come out to touch her; she reared away from him like a terrified animal. Her tear-washed face came out of the cushion, and in sheer self-preservation Annie Lacey surged furiously back to life. 'You've had what you wanted from me—now get out of here. *Get out*!'

Eyes as dark as the ocean beyond the window held onto stormy blue. He didn't flinch from the contempt she seared at him, did not respond to it. And for a moment out of time they stayed like that, he squatting there while she leaned accusingly towards him.

The damner being damned.

But even as she huddled there, flaying him with her eyes, she felt the lazy beginnings of other emotions start to flutter into corrupting life. Her pulse began to race, her aching breasts to stir, her senses pumping soft, sensual messages to the muscles around her sex.

His fault! He had done this to her—awoken demons she had believed so thoroughly shut away! And she hated him for that too, because it showed that no matter how degrading the revelation that had taken place in this room, she'd liked it, and wanted more.

Oh, God. 'Get out of here, you bastard,' she whispered thickly, and lowered her face again—though her senses were on full alert. Bastard he might be, but a proud one. And she was sure that he would not take kindly to having the word spat into his face.

Yet—he did take it; with only another heavy sigh he took it and drew himself grimly to his feet. 'At least get yourself into bed, Angelica,' he advised quietly. 'Or you will catch a chill sitting there like that. I will send Margarita up with some food.' He was walking towards the door. 'Perhaps by tomorrow you will be ready to talk. I will see you then.'

Annie waited until she heard the quiet click as the door closed behind him before she began crying all over again.

She was sitting on a rock, gazing emptily out to sea, when the skittering displacement of a pebble somewhere behind her warned her that she was no longer alone.

It was still quite early. Having surprisingly slept the sleep of the dead the night before, she had awoken just as dawn had been turning the sky from navy to blue. And on a restless urge to stop the events of the previous night from tumbling back into her head she'd got up, dressed in a simple pair of white shorts and a white T-shirt, then left her room via the French windows.

Glancing up, she saw César coming towards her. Barefoot, he moved easily across the light, pebbly ground, the solid gold bracelet of his watch glinting in the early morning light. Behind him his white-painted house stood in the shadow of a new day. Behind it stood the hill, with its thicket of trees reaching up towards a pure blue sky.

A beautiful place. Somewhere between Eden and paradise, she found herself thinking fancifully.

If César was the serpent Annie wasn't sure what that made her.

He was dressed in a light cambric shirt and a pair of thin white cotton beach trousers rolled up a little at the ankles. His hair was contained, his face wearing the sheen of a man who had just indulged in a close shave, and he looked devastatingly attractive.

A man who stood out on his own as special.

No. Firmly she squashed what was trying to take place inside her, and looked away again. She did not want to feel anything right now.

And she did not want to see the knowledge that she knew would be written in his shrewd emerald eyes if she let her own eyes clash with them.

He came to drop down beside her. No smile, no greeting—no tension in him. He simply drew up his knees, spread them slightly, rested his deeply tanned forearms on top, and said, 'Right. It is time for explanations, Angelica. I want to know what made you into the absolute fraud you are.'

Just like that. She smiled to herself. Guilt and remorse done with the night before, he now demanded enlightenment.

'Looking for absolution, Mr DeSanquez?' she asked. 'You won't get it, you know,' she warned him. 'All you will do is discover that you are just like the rest of the human race—rarely looking beyond what you're expecting to see.'

'And you with your carefully prepared persona did not aid that deception?' he countered.

Annie's shoulders moved in a careless shrug. 'I am in the business of selling things,' she reminded him.

'Using your notoriety to do it.'

'A commodity you weren't above exploiting yourself to help sell your precious collection. Which,' she added before he could say anything else, 'I accept entirely as part of my job. But it never occurred to you to look beyond the façade to the real person beneath.'

'It wasn't merely the false image which made you the woman I saw you to be, Angelica,' he argued. 'There were other, far more convincing factors which did that. Alvarez, for instance,' he prompted quietly.

'Alvarez', she noted. Luis Alvarez had suddenly become the detached 'Alvarez' instead of the more familiar 'brother-in-law'.

She almost smiled at the irony of it, only her stiff lips would not stretch to it. Instead she reached down to gather up a handful of pebbles from the side of her rock, then told him grimly, 'I am not going to bare my soul to you just because you've happened to discover my darkest secret.'

'It was not a dark secret, Angelica,' he countered gently. 'It was a sad one.'

Sad. A moment's moisture spread across her eyes then left again.

It was more than sad. It was pathetic, she thought bitterly as her mind flew back to that dark period in her life.

At sixteen years old she had to have been the most naïve female alive. A child actress with a fresh-faced, angelic image that had made people sigh when they'd seen her on their TV sets playing a role that had grown from a single ad for breakfast cereal into a three-year-long concept of how every parent would want their teenage daughter to look and behave.

The first ad had begun simply, with her sitting in a homely kitchen with the morning sunlight beaming down onto her pale gold head. She had been dressed for school in a neat lemon and white striped uniform and her face had shown the horrors that the voice-over had explained she was experiencing with the onset of her first day at a brand new school.

'Eat up,' her TV mother had commanded gently. 'Things won't look half so bad on a full stomach.'

Reluctantly she'd pulled the bowl of crunchy flakes towards her, dipped in her spoon and forced the first mouthful down; the next had not been quite so slow, the one after that almost eager. By the time she had finished the whole bowl her face had firmed, her small chin lifting determinedly, her thoughts—via the voice-over—having become more positive with each mouthful.

The next episode had shown her coming home again, buoyant, alive, rushing into the kitchen to tell her mother about her first exciting day, and all the time she'd chatted the bowl had been coming off the shelf, the crunchy-flake box out of the cupboard, milk from the fridge. Then had come the blissful silence as she'd eaten, blue eyes shining, the voice-over explaining her instant success at her new school as she'd replayed it to her bowl of cereal.

Over the next three years her crunchy cereal, via the voice-over discussions she'd had with it, had solved all her teenage problems with a lesson well learned at the end of each ad, which had earned her the nickname 'The Angel'.

The ads had been thrown up at other teenagers as perfect examples of good moral behaviour. She had been kind to animals, old people and small children. Parents had loved her, grandparents had loved her, small children had loved her—teenagers had hated her. Which was why she'd had so few friends of her own age—that and the fact that she'd lived with an aunt who had kept her strictly to heel when she had not been working or at school.

Losing Aunt Claire at the vulnerable age of nineteen had been like losing the linchpin that had held her un-natural life together. It had also preceded her spec-tacular fall from grace—a fall which had left her with two options only. Either she crawled away to hide in shame or she lifted her chin and outfaced everything that her critics had to throw at her. She had chosen the latter. And, with Todd's support, countless surprise offers had flooded in to Lissa, her agent, for the kind of work which must have made her aunt turn in her grave.

It was only as César's hand reached out to cover her own that she realised she was sitting there pressing damp pebbles between two tense palms as if she were trying to grind them into dust.

She looked down at that hand—big and dark, and seeming to promise so many things that she had learned not to trust. A hand that now knew her more intimately than any hand. The hand that had drawn from her a woman she hadn't known existed inside her.

The hand of contempt, now the hand of consolation.

She pushed it away.

There was a moment's silence, in which they both stared bleakly out to sea. Then, on a soft sigh that revealed an until now banked-down frustration, he requested brusquely, 'At least tell me what Hanson is to you.'

'Todd?' She turned a glance on him, seeing for the first time how his shattered illusions had scored deep grooves of strain into his lean, dark face. He was not so calm and composed, nor was he finished with guilt and remorse, she added as his eyes caught hers and held, the sombre glow of regret dulling the usual incisive greenness. 'Well, he's not my lover, that's for sure,' she drawled with mocking irreverence, watched him wince, then turned her face away again to stare back out to sea.

'He's my half-brother,' she announced.

Well aware that she had just delivered the biggest shock she could have done she selected one of the tiny pebbles in her hand and threw it into the ocean.

'We share the same father,' she extended, launching another pebble. 'Though I didn't find out about him until my aunt died.' She paused, then added, tight-lipped and flatly, 'Only she wasn't my aunt. She was my mother.'

Another stone was launched into the clear blue water while she gave those few pertinent facts a chance to settle in the stunned air now surrounding them. Then she quietly began relating a story that she had never told anyone in her life before—though why she suddenly chose to tell this man was beyond her ability to understand.

'Not once during the eighteen years I lived with her did she ever let me know that interesting little fact,' she told him. 'I had to wait until she was dead to discover our true relationship—via letters sent from Todd's father to her, laying out ground rules for the lump sum he settled on us both which involved her holding her silence about his name. Why she decided to include herself in that silence I don't know.' And will never know now, she added bleakly to herself. 'But discovering that far from being the orphan I'd always believed myself to be I'd had not only a mother but a father as well sent me a little crazy for a time.'

'You were hurt,' he defended her gently.

'And the rest,' she said, and huffed out a sound of scorn. Hurt, angry, bitter, betrayed.

She hunched her body over her knees, a fresh handful of pebbles clenched in her fist.

'I stormed into Giles Hanson's office and began shrieking at him like a maniac,' she went on after a moment. 'I accused him of just about everything I could accuse him of, then set about telling him what I thought of him as a man.'

The word 'man' emerged with enough contempt to make any man wince. César winced.

'I had just got to the part where I was telling him how I was going to reveal to the world how he and my mother had treated me when Todd came into the room.'

She turned to look at him then, her gaze skimming over his set, sober face. 'Your eyes are the same colour as Susie's,' she remarked—quite out of context. 'I should have made that connection a lot earlier than I did. And I'm surprised now that I didn't.'

He glanced at her frowningly, not really understanding what she was getting at. 'We have nothing else